THE HUNTER SECRET

RITE WORLD: BLACKTHORN HUNTERS ACADEMY
BOOK 2

JULIANA HAYGERT

COPYRIGHT

AUTHOR'S NOTE

I hope you enjoy reading *The Hunter Secret*!

Don't forget to sign up for my Newsletter to find out about new releases, cover reveals, giveaways, and more!

If you want to see exclusive teasers, help me decide on covers, read excerpts, talk about books, etc, join my reader group on Facebook: Juliana's Club!

RITE WORLD

Welcome to the RITE WORLD!

Free Novella:
The Vampire Hunt

Rite World:
The Vampire Heir (Book 1)
The Witch Queen (Book 2)
The Immortal Vow (Book 3)
The Warlock Lord (Book 4)
The Wolf Consort (Book 5)
The Crystal Rose (Book 6)
The Wolf Forsaken (Book 7)
The Fae Bound (Book 8)
The Blood Pact (Book 9)

Rite World: Blackthorn Hunters Academy
The Demons Kiss (Book 1)

The Hunter Secret (Book 2)
The Soul Bond (Book 3)
The Shadow Trials (Book 4)
The Immortal Vow (Book 5)

And more to come!

THE VAMPIRE HUNT

I have an exclusive novella set in the Rite World that is just for my newsletter subscribers!

Click here to sign-up and receive your book!

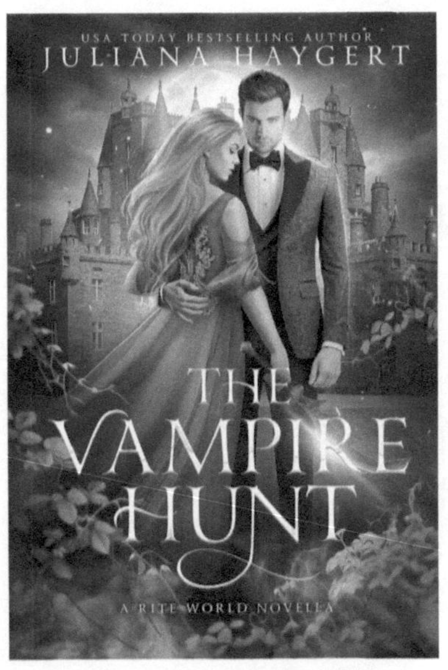

THE VAMPIRE HUNT
A Rite World Novella

Norah is a demon hunter, one of the best graduated from the Blackthorn Hunters Academy. When she's sent to investigate a case concerning demons in a small town, she runs into a very arrogant vampire. Her first instinct is to kill him, after all, he's a supernatural and demon hunters are taught to end all evil.

Cain is a vampire prince. Because of his status, he's in charge of making sure humans don't find out about his kind. During a routine investigation, he bumps into a very sexy demon hunter and he wonders what she's doing on his way.

However, the case grows much bigger for Norah and Cain to handle alone. To find the truth and win this battle, the vampire and the demon hunter will have to hunt together—without killing each other.

How well could this end?

MAP

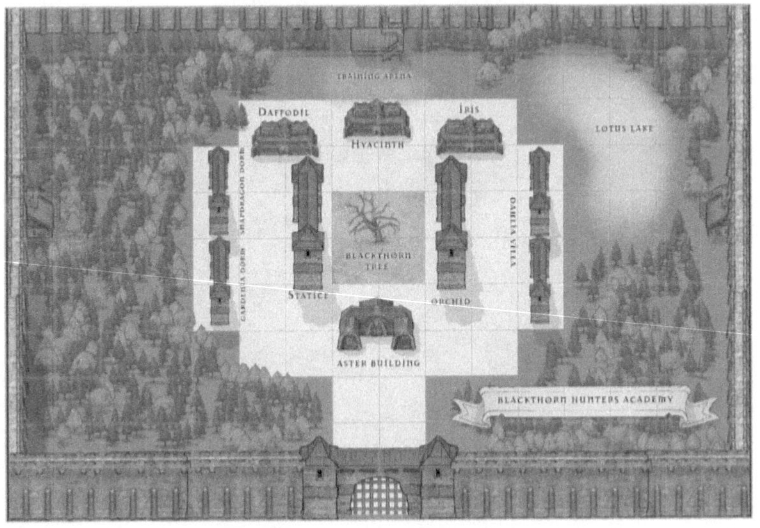

Map of Blackthorn Hunters Academy

Click here to view the map in a separate browser.

1

ERIN

MY LIFE CHANGED COMPLETELY FIVE MONTHS AGO.

I grabbed another shirt from my closet and shoved it inside the bag on my bed. Even these ... this shirt, this closet, this bag, this bed—they were all new. Five months ago, I would have never dreamed of this crazy freaking life.

But things were what they were. I couldn't deny it anymore. I was half demon hunter and the half-demon daughter of the stoic Professor Martha and Brikan, the king of the underworld. And because of it, my mother thought everything would go downhill from here.

To me, everything started going downhill the day I entered the haunted house on a dare and my aunt Paula died, but the biggest turn of all had been when I found out about my father—and when Rey and I had made a deal with the headmaster, Randall.

In the last month of classes before the end of the fall semester, the headmaster had summoned me. If he had summoned Rey, I didn't know. To be honest, I didn't know anything about Rey anymore. After that kiss—that amazing, breathtaking kiss—he told me he had no interest in me and he distanced himself from me. He even convinced Professor Astrid to let him change class periods. I ended up without a partner in weapons forging class and I almost failed.

Despite the immense sadness I had felt the first week when I didn't see or hear from Rey, I forced myself to move on. To forget about him. He didn't like me? That was okay. It wasn't the end of the world. I was only nineteen. I was in no rush to find love or have a serious relationship. I liked being single and spending time with Claire.

Speaking of Claire ...

I glanced at the time on my cell phone sitting on the nightstand. Claire should be arriving any time now. She promised to come here the moment she was back. I narrowed my eyes, wondering if I could sneak a phone call before my mother caught me using my phone. Cell phones were forbidden at the academy. Last semester, I had had mine in my bedroom with me, because I didn't have anywhere to keep it, but this time, my mother wanted me to leave it here. Would I be able to?

I reached for my phone.

"Erin?"

I whipped to the door. "Claire?"

A moment later, my friend stepped into my room. "I'm back!" Short brown curls bouncing, she opened her arms and rushed to me. "I missed you." She squeezed me tight.

I chuckled, trying to return the hug, but not able to when she tackled me like this. "Me too."

She pulled back and smiled at me, her green eyes twinkling. "It's so good to be back." She plopped down on my bed beside my bag. "Holy crap, you have no idea how bored I was."

I snorted. Professor Crimson, Claire's father, had taken her to visit his mother, a retired demon hunter living in Chasseur Ville, just a few minutes from here. But because Professor Crimson had a stick up his butt, he hadn't let Claire take her phone or send any kind of news to me during winter break.

"I wasn't bored," I told her, "but I bet it wasn't much better either."

"Ha, I might take on that bet. Can you imagine? My grandmother is as rigid and demanding as my father. For the last two weeks, all I heard was about how I had to work harder and do better to uphold the family name." Her shoulders slumped. "We all know I'll never be the demon hunter they want me to."

I poked my foot at her ankle. "I can help you."

She rolled her eyes. "I doubt that, but you're welcome to try." I picked up another shirt from my closet and put it in my bag. Claire's eyes softened. "How about you? How has it been?"

I glanced around the bedroom. Students weren't expected to stay in the dorms during winter break and summer vacation. When the semester ended, I had no idea where to go. As far as I knew, the house I lived in with my aunt had been sold. With that money, I could rent a place nearby, but the last couple of times I had been by myself outside the academy walls, I had been attacked by demons. I wasn't sure I wanted to repeat that.

Professor Martha surprised me when she invited me to stay at her house.

"I'm your mother," she said in her robot-like voice. She wasn't as bad as Professor Crimson, but she sure wasn't open either. "It's only right for you to move in with me."

I was skeptical at first, but what other choice did I have? So, I crossed the campus to the Dahlia Villa and joined my mother at her townhouse. Matching my mother's personality, the townhouse interior decoration was contemporary and impeccable, with nothing out of place. I couldn't imagine myself lounging on the leather couch, eating popcorn, with my feet on the glass coffee table. Or devouring a pizza with my hands at the sleek dining room.

As we moved around the townhouse, I realized it was bigger than I first realized, with spare rooms that had been turned into an office and library and guest bedrooms. I thought she would put me in one of those, but then she took me to the last door on the second floor. To my surprise, this bedroom was different. It reminded me of my room at the academy: twin bed, nightstand, desk and chair, dresser, and a walk-in closet and bathroom, but here the wood was white and the accents—blanket, curtains, etc.—were light blue and off-white. Simple, clean, but pretty and cozy.

"This is your bedroom," she said, beckoning me to enter. "Though the decorations have changed over the years, this has always been your room."

I stared at her, speechless.

Moments like those wreak havoc inside of me, but they were rare. Instead of having a nice, lazy break where I got to know my mother and spend my first Christmas and New Year with her, we spent most of the time in the basement. Doing what? Training.

It was all about training.

Protesting didn't help, so after a while, I gave up. It would be easy to just suck it up and go through her intense training regimen than try to rebel. Try being the key word. She would never allow me to rebel.

"It has been ... odd," I confessed. I told her about training nonstop and no bonding time whatsoever. "I guess it's better than being out there alone." At least, that was what I told myself.

My feelings regarding my mother were messed up. I still resented her for abandoning me and for being so cold and distant, but despite it all, I understood her reasons. I knew why she kept away; it was to protect me. That had to count for something, right?

In my head, I called her my mother, since it was easier and felt better than calling her professor. However, I couldn't bring myself to call her my mother out loud. Whenever I had to talk to her, I either called her professor, or simply Martha. Thankfully, she didn't push the subject—not that I thought she would.

"I'm sure she'll warm up to you in no time," Claire said. "After all, everything she did was for you, to save you. That means she loves you a lot."

I frowned. That might be true in theory, but it was hard to believe it when she was so cold to me. I let out a long breath. "It doesn't matter now." I shoved a jacket in my bag and zipped it up.

A slow smile tugged at Claire's lips. "Nothing else happened? Nothing interesting?"

"What do you mean?"

Her smile widened. "Like ... Rey. Didn't he come to see you?"

I scoffed. She knew very well that Rey had shut me out completely after our kiss in the graveyard. She also knew my feelings for him had only grown in the meantime. I was so stupid. "Why would he?"

"Because he realized he loved you and needed you."

"Right," I drawled.

I pulled my shirt out, threw it on the floor, and picked up a clean one from the closet.

"Oh!" Claire yelled, startling me. "I did some research during the break." She pointed to my chest. "I know now what that mark means."

I glanced down at myself. Some time ago, a mark appeared above my heart—a small black mark that looked like two sideway hearts entwined, tied together by another swirly line. When I first noticed it, it was right after the battle at the cemetery. My urge was to find Rey and tell him about it. He knew what the mark on my wrist meant; he would know what this one meant. But since his disappearing act, I let that idea go. So, I asked Claire during class one day. She said that mark was familiar, but she couldn't remember from where. We had plans to research it, but then the final exams hit us hard and Claire became a studying robot. I thought about researching it on my own, but to be honest, I was afraid of the meaning.

The first one was a sign marking me as the daughter of the king of the underworld. This one couldn't be much better, could it?

But apparently, after the stress of finals and going to visit her grandmother, Claire remembered.

"Do I want to know?" I asked, pulling a clean shirt over my head. The mark was pretty, just like a small, delicate tattoo over my left breast, but that didn't mean I liked to look at it.

"I knew I had seen it before," she said, her voice eager. "It's the sign of a soul bond."

"A soul what?"

"A soul bond," she said, as if I should know what that

meant. "A soul bond is the connection formed when twin souls find each other. Technically, it's called a Twin Soul Bond." Her eyes shone. "That means you've found your soulmate."

"What?" I shrieked.

Claire's nose wrinkled. "If it's not Rey, who could it be? Harvey, maybe?"

"Claire, what the hell? That doesn't make sense. A soulmate? Me? Don't you think I would know?" I gestured to my chest. "This can't mean that."

"But it does." She stood. "I would say someone at the academy is your true love. Now you just have to find him. He's sure to have the same mark in the same exact place."

"No way." I shook my head. "I don't want to find a soulmate. I don't want any bond connecting me to someone. I'm fine by myself."

"This isn't up to you," she said. "From what I read, your twin soul calls for you. Sooner or later, you'll find it."

This subject irritated me. The only guy on my mind and in my heart was Rey, but he had shut me out. If he was my soulmate, if he felt for me the same way I felt for him, he wouldn't have told me he didn't like me. He wouldn't have pushed me away.

Right?

I shook my head again, determined to forget about this nonsense. "All right, that's enough." I grabbed a thick sweater from my closet and put it on. "Are you ready to go?"

Claire nodded. "My bags are on the porch."

After putting on my thick black wool coat over the sweater, I slung one of my bags across my shoulders and picked up the duffel from the floor. Many of my things had stayed in my dorm room across campus, like the picture of my aunt and me, her Dawnblade, and my uniforms. But even so, it wasn't like I needed a bunch of things. And if I forgot something, it was easy to come back to my mother's house and grab it.

Together, Claire and I trailed to the front of the townhouse. As I expected, my mother was nowhere to be seen. Since classes started the next day, I bet she was in her office in the Aster building, getting ready for the new semester.

Outside, the chilly wind whipped around, ruffling my hair. "At least, it's not snowing anymore," I said with a groan. It had snowed most of the winter break. The paths between the buildings had been cleared, but the amount of snow accumulated in the grass and at the corners of the buildings reached my thighs.

My entire life, Aunt Paula and I had moved a lot. The best places we had lived were Florida and southern California, where it was warm year-round. When we moved to Colorado a few years ago, I protested. She assured me I would get used to the snow and ice. Well, I hadn't, and I doubted I ever would.

Though the snow had been shoveled away, the pathways were still slick, so Claire and I walked slowly across the campus, toward the Gardenia building, which housed the female dorm.

As we crossed the square in the middle of campus, I stared at the big Blackthorn tree. In the middle of so much snow, the tree seemed to have a dark glow, its thousands of thorns shining like jewels. It was so beautiful and yet so dark, so cold, so eerie.

Claire and I weren't the only ones arriving at the Gardenia building. Many students walked into the dorms, carrying bags and boxes. In the Snapdragon building next to Gardenia, the boys did the same.

Claire and I split once we arrived on the second floor. I fished the keys from my coat pocket and unlocked the door to my room. Then, I kicked the door open and threw my duffel bag on the floor.

"Home, sweet home," I whispered, glancing around.

Though it had been only two weeks, it seemed like I hadn't been here in forever. Despite being grateful that my mother had taken me in during the winter break, her house would never feel like mine. This room felt more like home than anywhere else I had lived so far.

With a sigh, I took off my coat and started organizing my things. After making sure everything I had left behind was intact, that my uniforms and boots were clean, I unpacked my bags and placed my clothes inside my closet.

I was almost done when a knock came from the door.

Frowning, I glanced at the closed door. If it was Claire, she would have tried opening the door, which was unlocked, before knocking. Who else could be coming for me? Ava? Harvey? I doubted it.

Rey?

Yeah, right.

Shaking my head, I opened the door.

"Hey," Rey said, standing in the middle of the hallway.

I stared at him, stunned. I really hadn't expected it to be him. But, holy shit, I had forgotten how beautiful he was. Well, not really, but damn, could he get more handsome each time I saw him? Tall, with just the right amount of bulk, a handsome face full of sharp angles, and brilliant gray eyes that sometimes looked silver—he was the exact definition of eye candy.

His beauty plus the way he stood, so sure of himself, so powerful, so intimidating, had my heart tugging inside my chest.

I frowned. "Hm, what are you doing here?"

"Randall wants us."

My frown deepened. The headmaster hadn't sent for me in almost two months. I had barely set foot back into the dorms and he was suddenly breathing down my neck. "Right now?" I asked, skeptical.

Rey nodded. "Right now."

I stared at him some more. Here was the guy who made my heart skip a beat. The guy who had ignored me for a couple of months now. The guy who apparently wasn't my soulmate.

I wouldn't admit it out loud, but that hurt so bad.

Impatience dripped from him as he turned the collar of his thick black coat up, giving him a regal air. A powerful stance. A heartbreaking sight.

Knowing this could only end badly, I grabbed my coat from my chair. "All right. Let's go."

2

REY

The Dark Creek Pub never seemed so fucking boring.

This winter break had been brutal on all accounts: It didn't stop snowing; demons who had been loyal to Asmodeus were coming after me left and right, trying to avenge my father—as if I had been the one to kill him; my drinking buddy, Wyatt, was nowhere to be found; and the mark on my chest seemed to itch and burn sometimes.

I brought the beer bottle to my lips and—

Fuck, I had drunk all of it already. With my half-demon metabolism, I didn't get drunk easily, but I could say I was almost drunk now. It took only nine bottles.

I could definitely use a tenth.

I lifted my hand to call the waitress when my phone rang. I pulled it from my pocket and glanced at it.

Randall's name flashed on the screen.

The motherfucker hadn't called me all winter break, and now, one day before classes started, he remembered I existed. I wish he would forget I existed altogether.

Maybe then our magical contract would be nulled. Just like that.

Only in my fucking dreams.

I rubbed at where the soul bond mark was stamped on my chest. Soul bonds could be used to break demonic contracts, but my contract with Randall wasn't demonic. I couldn't even use that for my advantage now.

I answered the phone. "Yes?"

"Be in my office with Erin in exactly two hours," Randall said, his voice sharp.

"Yes—"

He ended the call.

I groaned, wishing I could tell him to go to hell.

I knew I would have to face Erin at some point, but I hoped it would be later. Much later.

I also had hoped Randall had forgotten about his deal with her. That he had done it only to scare her.

No such luck.

Hope and luck. Two useless things that I should scratch off my fucking dictionary.

After paying for my binge drinking, I walked out of the pub. I inhaled the cold air, willing it to clear my mind, to push the drunkenness away. I had two hours to sober up.

I stopped by the motel I had been crashing at, took a cold shower, drank an entire bottle of water, got dressed, and left the motel to go back to the only place that felt like home.

After walking into a dark alley, I shifted into a raven and flew to the academy. Several times during winter break, I had regretted leaving my car at the academy, but now I was glad I didn't have to worry about it. By car, it would have taken me five hours to get there. In my raven form, it took less than one.

The flight in the cold air also helped send the last of my inebriation away.

When I arrived at the academy, students swarmed the Gardenia and the Snapdragon buildings—getting back to their dorms. I had no idea how my room looked right now. Probably messy and full of dust; I had left in a hurry once classes had ended last semester. The faster I left the academy, the less chance I had of bumping into Erin.

Which was ridiculous since now I was walking directly to her room.

When Erin opened the door and saw me, it was like she was staring at a ghost. Her shock didn't take away from her beauty though. She was so fucking beautiful, even when looking at me with her guard up.

I tried sounding and looking unaffected, as if seeing her after so long didn't bother me at all. As if I still felt nothing for her.

That was fucking hard.

I pulled the collar of my coat up, like another wall around me. Clearly irritated, Erin grabbed her jacket and said, "All right. Let's go."

Quiet, she followed me out of the Gardenia building, down the slippery stone paths, and into the Aster building. All the way, I had braced myself, expecting her to say something, to ask something, to start a conversation, but she had barely glanced my way.

Which was good. Really good.

But it fucking hurt.

Although the soul bond mark didn't cause pain, I was certain I could feel it. It was like a string, pulling me to Erin. An arrow, turning me to her. Several times during the winter break, I had to physically stop myself from coming after her, from checking on her, just to make sure she was okay.

But I knew she was okay. Professor Martha would never let anything happen to her. I had nothing to fear.

And yet, I couldn't stop worrying. She was the daughter of the fucking king of the underworld, a demonic princess set to inherit his kingdom. It was only a matter of time before he came after her himself.

That wasn't the only thing worrying me. After Asmodeus's death, I was targeted as a traitor. The entire underworld was after me, to deliver me on a silver platter to the king. If word got out that Erin was my soulmate, that she shared the twin soul bond with me, she wouldn't only be taken to the king. She would be used to lure me in.

I couldn't let them use her that way.

I had to keep a safe distance from her in order to protect her.

Unfortunately, Randall had another idea.

Once we entered his office, Randall ordered us to take the seats across from his desk. The immortal demon hunter smiled at us, a fake grin I was used to. With his ageless look, his gray hair, and warm dark eyes, Randall almost looked like a caring man.

He didn't fool me.

"I have a special mission for the two of you," he announced, a small hint of excitement in his voice.

I frowned. "What do you mean, for the two of us?"

"You'll be working together on this," he said.

"I don't think that's such a great idea," I protested.

Beside me, Erin flinched.

Randall lost his amused grin. "I don't care what you think. I'm telling you what is going to happen." He steepled his long fingers over his desk. "You two will search for other half-demons, so we can create a special group."

"Other half-demons?" I asked, pondering. Of course, I knew Erin and I weren't the only ones out there, but what could Randall possibly want with more half-demons?

Erin sat straighter. "What are you going to do with them?"

"Don't worry," Randall said, his voice flat. "Just like you two seem to have the best interest of the demon hunters' affairs at heart, I want to find other half-demons with the same ideals, to welcome them into the academy."

Erin shook her head. "The other students, their parents, and even the professors will be against that."

"That's why we'll keep it a secret for now," Randall said. "But with time, I want to reduce the prejudice against half-demons and create a special program for them here at the academy."

I opened my mouth to protest, to tell him this was a crazy dream that would never happen, but when he cut me a look that told me it wasn't open for discussion, I pressed my lips together.

"Where do we start?" I asked instead.

Erin cut me a wide-eyed look. I ignored her.

"I know there are other half-demons in the school and in the nearby towns," Randall said. "Your job is to find them and get them to join the Black Knight Unit, which will be our half-demon force."

"How will we find them?" I asked.

"With this," Randall said, pulling a silver-chain necklace from a drawer. The chain was long, with a plain, round silver pendant, much like an old coin. He handed the necklace to Erin. "Wear this."

Brow furrowed, Erin took the necklace, but hesitated before putting it on. "What now?" she asked.

"The amulet will warn you when there's any half-demon in the area." He pushed a leather pouch across his desk. "Here are more amulets like that. Give one to each of the half-demons you find."

I took the pouch, glad he didn't insist I wear one.

Erin glanced at the amulet hanging from her neck. "What if they don't want to join us?"

"Then you report them to me," Randall said. "I'll take care of them." *Take care of them.* I didn't like that. He continued, "I'll leave it to you two. Come up with the plans, strategize, and go after them." He lifted a finger as if remembering something. "One important thing: Do not tell anyone about this."

Since Randall knew I was good at keeping secrets, that seemed like a warning for Erin. What, was he afraid she would tell Professor Martha about it? Or maybe Claire, and Claire would tell her father, Professor Crimson?

"We won't," I said, hoping Erin understood what he meant.

Randall leaned back in his chair. "I want a report in one week."

That was his way of dismissing us.

I shot up from my seat. "Yes, sir."

Erin hesitated, but mimicked me and stood up. She dragged her feet behind me as I left the office and closed the door.

Once we reached the staircase, the words flew out of her mouth. "You're kidding me, right?"

I climbed down the steps, not looking at her. "What do you mean?"

"Half-demons," she whispered. "In the school? That's not a good idea."

I knew that, but what could I do? I was the slave obeying my master's wishes. I had no control over what I could do, or what I couldn't. Unfortunately, she was in that same boat.

I stopped in the middle of the stairs and turned to her. "You'll soon realize that when you make a deal like ours, you don't have a choice."

Erin almost bumped into me. She took a step back and frowned at me. "Then we should make him understand and change his mind."

A hollow chuckle escaped my lips. "Dream on."

I resumed walking.

"Hey!" she called, but I ignored her. I heard her humph and the stomping of her feet as she trailed after me. "There he goes, ignoring me again," she muttered.

Holy fuck, did she even know how much it hurt to ignore her? To ignore the feelings swirling inside me, screaming at me that she was the one? That there was no one else for me? That I loved her?

But I couldn't have her.

I shouldn't.

Outside the building, I braced myself and turned to her. Hands inside the pockets of her coat, Erin stopped in front of me.

"Erin, when Randall said you can't tell anyone, he was serious," I told her. I had had a contract hanging over my head for almost a thousand years. I knew the consequences of disobeying even the mildest of the orders. "You can't tell anyone. Not your mother. Not even Claire."

She frowned. "Why?"

"Just ... you can't, all right. Trust me."

She muttered "trust me" under her breath, as if she thought that was funny. Then, she let out a long breath and asked, "What now? Should we make a list of the students who we think could be half-demons too?"

Yes, we should, but I wasn't going to hang around her any more than necessary.

"We can do that alone," I said, before turning my back to her and walking away.

Fuck, I sounded like a jerk. But if that was the way for her to be safe, then so be it. I would be the biggest jerk of all.

3

ERIN

My mother swiped her leg. Because of the stance I was in—from having just landed a roundhouse kick to her side—I didn't have time to move away or jump back.

I ended up on the floor, with the air knocked out from my lungs.

My mother leaned over me, her hands on her waist. Before I found out she was my mother, I hadn't noticed how similar we look. The same long, thick, black hair, the same sharp eyebrows, the same thin nose. My eye shape also looked like hers, just her eyes were hazel, while mine were an odd gold color. She wasn't too tall and slim built like me, but packed with muscles. I liked to believe that if I kept up with this intense training, I would become as hard as a rock too.

"You've got to be faster." She extended her hand to me. When we first started training together, she didn't help me get up. Instead, she threw more weight on me and expected me to find a way to get free. "Most demons are faster than us."

And demon hunters were already fast. At least, faster than humans. One thing I did notice since we began training together was my demon hunter side coming out—my increased speed, my superior strength. I was still average when compared to the other demon hunters, but I sure was faster and stronger than any other human I had met.

I grabbed her hand and she tugged me up. "I'm trying," I told her. "I'm already faster than I was six months ago."

She nodded. "I know."

One thing that hadn't changed this semester was our early morning training sessions. It was the freaking first day of class, and my mother had already dragged me to the Hyacinth building. At least I had convinced her to train at five-thirty instead of five. I wanted to get every spare minute of sleep I could.

I glanced at the big round clock on the wall. It was almost seven. If I wanted to take a shower and have breakfast before my first class, it was time to go. I picked up my towel from the mat. "We're done, right?"

"We are," she said.

I frowned. "I can hear a but there."

My mother fixed her eyes on mine. "I know the headmaster asked to see you and Rey yesterday afternoon. What did he want?"

Shit. I honestly didn't mind telling her, but I didn't want to disobey Randall. After all, he was the headmaster, and I now had a deal with him. He had ordered Rey and me not to tell anyone about our special mission. I bet that included my mother.

"I can't tell you," I confessed. If I lied and told her crap, she would eventually find out and give me a hard time about it. I would rather argue now and be done with it. "He told us to keep quiet about it."

Last night, I sat at my desk and started the list of possible half-demons at the school, but I didn't get too far. I only knew most of the students in the second year and some from the third with whom I had some elective classes last semester. The others, I might have seen around campus, but I didn't know their names. Unfortunately, I would need Rey's help for this.

"I don't like this," she muttered. She took two steps, closing most of the distance between us. I stood still, glad I wasn't wearing the amulet the headmaster had given me. "If he tells you to do something dangerous, you come to me. You don't need to tell me what it is, if you can't, but tell me to come along, to help you. I want to help you."

A lump rose in my throat. Why she was so considerate sometimes? "I will," I told her to appease her. Hopefully, the headmaster wouldn't send me on any dangerous missions.

After that, I gathered my coat and ran back to the dorm. It was frigid outside, but because I had been exercising, it didn't really feel too bad. Until I took a shower, ate breakfast, and had to face the cold outside in my uniform—a white shirt and green tie, a think black jacket, pleated skirt, and tights. I had bought the thickest tights I could find, but with the freezing cold outside, they were still not enough.

Right now, I envied the male students who could wear pants.

At least, we could put on black coats over our clothes. Unfortunately, mine went down to my thighs. As I made my way to the Orchid building, I made a mental note to buy a coat that went down to my feet. That ought to help.

On my way, I saw many faces I knew: Harvey and Peter, Ava with Stella and Ruby, and even Harper. They were all second-year students like me. But it seemed none of them had the same classes I did, because they entered at the Statice building, while I went on. I hadn't seen Claire this morning, and because we weren't able to schedule all the same classes, I wouldn't see her until later this morning.

Feeling a little down, I entered the classroom for demonic anthropology and took a seat along the wall. What could this class be about?

Professor Vander entered the room and started the lecture without even saying hello or telling us more about the semester and his class. What the hell?

But his subject was interesting.

"We know of eight princes of the underworld," he said. The tall man with oddly long legs and bald head moved his hands in circles as he spoke. "Princes Paimon, Maggoth, Zeltov, Aymon, Artonth, Toriens, Ergin, and Asmodeus." He paused, looking around the room. "As you all know, our beloved headmaster, Randall Boucher, killed Prince Asmodeus in November last year."

A student raised her hand. I had seen her around last semester, but I honestly didn't remember her name. "Professor, will you tell us more about that? All we heard was that Asmodeus ambushed the headmaster and was killed."

"I'm sure the headmaster would have already told us more details if there were any," Professor Vander said. I kept quiet, of course. If the headmaster didn't want to tell anyone about what happened, I certainly didn't mind. "Anyway, there are people who believe there are more princes in the underworld who we don't know about."

Another girl raised her hand. "Professor, I thought we weren't supposed to learn about the princes until the fourth year."

"The curriculum is changing and we're introducing princes sooner now," the professor said. "Don't make us regret this choice." He cleared his throat. "As I was saying," he went on with the lecture as if his answer was a satisfying one.

Mildly amused with the class subject, I flipped through the book and saw sketches of the demons. Even the princes had sketches and I was surprised to see Asmodeus's sketch was fairly accurate. I flipped to the next page, where a picture of Prince Paimon was displayed. For some time last year, we had believed Prince Paimon had been the one after me. He might have been, but it was only because he was King Brikan's favorite prince and the king had sent him after me.

I sighed and flipped some more pages, searching for a section about—

There. An entire chapter on King Brikan.

The chapter opened explaining how King Brikan rose to power, by killing the other original demons, and how he created the princes to do his bidding. Then, it went on about how he had ruled for centuries and throughout many civilizations, including ancient Egypt, the Roman empire, the English monarchy, and many more.

Apparently, King Brikan had been involved in a lot of wars around the world, and was responsible for major catastrophes.

My stomach dropped.

And I was the daughter of this freaking demon.

Well, perhaps this was good. This class, I meant. Perhaps in here I would learn a thing or two about King Brikan. I would learn more about my connection to him, and maybe even how I could defeat him if he came for me.

Ha, what a dream. Me defeating an almighty king of the underworld? Not even in my dreams ...

I was so entranced in reading about King Brikan that I didn't even notice the time passing. We were dismissed from class, and I picked up my things and went to meet with Claire for our free period. During the warmer months, we liked to sit in the square and look at the Blackthorn tree, but in the winter, we stayed in the cafeteria or media room.

She was already waiting for me in the cafeteria with two Styrofoam cups of sweet hot chocolate when I got there.

"I love you," I told her.

Claire winked at me. "I know."

I sat down on a bench around a round table beside her, took my warm cup in my freezing hands, and looked out the glass walls to the winter land around campus. From here, we couldn't see much. Only the pathways, the Statice building, and lots of snow. Students walked by, going to and from classes.

"Isn't it odd to be back?" I asked. I was feeling odd, at least. This place was home, but at the same time, I felt like I didn't deserve it. I was a half-demon ... and not only that, I was daughter of the Supreme Demon. At first, I had trouble wrapping my mind around it, but during the last two months, I came to realize that denying it wouldn't change the truth. I was a demonic princess and my father would come for me.

Which made me wonder, should I run again? If I stayed here, I would only be putting others in danger. Claire, my mother, Rey, and the other students. If I left, if I went far away, they would be safe.

"Not to me," Claire said. "Even though I'm only in my second year, this place has been my home for a long time now." Right. I kept forgetting her father had been a professor here for many years, and she had been raised at the academy. "But I can honestly say it's better now that I have a best friend." She smiled at me.

I smiled back at her. "I don't know how you put up with me."

She bumped her shoulder on mine. "What do you mean? You're pretty, you're smart, and you're fun. Plus—" She leaned closer and lowered her voice. "—you're super interesting with your half-demon blood and demonic princess legacy."

"Shhh." I glanced around, afraid someone would hear us, but there were only a few people in the cafeteria and they weren't close to us. "That isn't interesting. It's screwed up."

She shrugged. "At least it's never boring."

I snorted. Well, in a way, she was right. So far, things had been complicated and a little dangerous. If life kept being never-boring, we were sure to encounter even worse problems.

Speaking of problems, I remembered the half-demons list I was supposed to make. I wanted to talk to Claire about it. She knew everyone at the academy, even past and upcoming students, but the headmaster had told us to stay quiet about this task.

Before I could make up my mind to tell her, a shadow fell over us. When I turned my head to see who had approached us, I almost dropped my hot chocolate.

"Rey," I whispered, in shock. What was the deal with this guy? Yesterday, he dismissed me, and now here he was, right in front of me. I braced myself, and my voice sounded a lot harsher when I asked, "What do you want?"

"Hi, Rey," Claire said in a friendly tone, totally ignoring my question. "How was your winter break?"

Rey frowned. "Hm, it was okay." He buried his hands inside his coat's pockets. "This morning I realized we never got to close the demon portal."

"Holy crap, you're right!" Claire sat straighter. "And that was what? Two months ago?"

Rey nodded. "Yeah. There have been a few demon sightings around the mountain, so I was thinking we should close it."

"We?" I asked, lost. "Why we? You can do it by yourself."

"Erin!" Claire exclaimed.

Rey fixed his gray eyes on mine. "I can't. I need your help."

This was amusing. The guy who had shut me down last night was now coming to me for help. "*My* help? Why is that?"

"I'm not strong enough alone," he said, his tone even. If my harshness was getting to him, he hid it well. "I need your magic added to mine."

I held his stare, but didn't say anything. In my mind, I understood what he was saying. We should close the portal so it would be harder for demons to get closer to the school. That was in my interest too. But I was still upset with him, and because of it, I wanted him to suffer too.

"Erin," Claire whispered. "You have to do it."

I sighed. "Fine."

"Good," he said, still sounding like a robot.

"Are we using the same spell?" Claire asked. "Do you need me to bring the ingredients again?"

Rey shook his head. "No, we won't need a special ritual or ingredients to do this."

"Oh, all right." Claire's shoulders deflated. It was as if she wanted to be more active in our quests, poor girl.

Rey took a step back. "We'll meet here tonight and go out to the portal."

Then he whipped around and left.

Claire fake-glared at me. "Did you need to be such a bitch?"

I gasped. "Me? A bitch? He's the one who told me off last night and now he wants my help."

"What?" Claire narrowed her eyes. "You saw him last night?" She slapped my arm. "How dare you not tell me?"

I curled into myself, protecting my body from her assault. "It wasn't a big deal. He had a message from the headmaster, and then wouldn't talk to me again," I said, changing the truth a little bit.

"Oh crap, there's more to the story." If Claire was a dog, her ears would have perked up. "Tell me more."

"There's nothing to tell." I sipped from my hot chocolate, thinking of what to say. "The headmaster just sent a note welcoming me back to the academy."

"What about your deal?"

My eyes scanned the area again, but no one was close. Still, I kept my voice low when I said, "The headmaster still hasn't sent for me," I lied. Shit, I hated lying to her. I seriously had to measure if I could tell her all about the headmaster and his first mission or not, but it wouldn't be now. Now, we had to finish our drinks and go to our next class. "Ready for class?"

She smiled at me. "Always."

4

REY

WHEN I FIRST REALIZED WE HADN'T CLOSED THAT FUCKING portal, I thought about doing it alone. If I wanted to keep Erin safe, it was imperative that the portal was closed right away. I had even gone out there again and tried to do it, but I couldn't. I was strong, but not strong enough to close it alone. I needed help.

The only other people I knew who had magic at the academy were Randall and Erin. I didn't want to bring it up to Randall, so my only choice was to ask Erin. As a demonic princess, she was sure to be strong. The question was, could she access all that power?

When I arrived in the cafeteria, I thought about grabbing coffee for us, like I used to do when Erin and I trained late at night last semester. Then, I stopped myself. Yes, I wanted to get fucking coffee for Erin, but damn, I couldn't. I shouldn't.

So, I just stayed put and waited.

It didn't take long for her and Claire to arrive.

"Do you still have Professor Martha's pass?" I asked Erin.

She fished it out of her coat pocket, showed it to me, then

stored it away. The way she was talking—or not talking—to me upset me. It got under my skin, but I did my best to ignore it because it was for the best. If she wasn't talking to me, it meant I had hurt her. If I had hurt her, she would keep her distance from me.

But not tonight.

I swear, if I could have used anyone else's help for this fucking spell, I would have. But there was no one else. Only Erin.

Once more, I had created a small interval between the guard change at the northeast outpost, and we used that opportunity to sneak out of the academy. The way to the portal was quiet and slow. The moon's ambient light reflected off the snow, making it eerily bright for a late night. The snow hadn't accumulated much beneath the clusters of trees, but it still made the trek a lot harder than it could have been.

I couldn't help but steal glances at Erin and Claire. Lately, I hadn't seen Claire without two or more books under her arm. Tonight was no different. She had a tote bag slung over her shoulder and three leather-bound books peeking from the opening.

As for Erin, she stomped in the snow with her thick boots, her arms crossed in front of her chest, and her brows curled down. I wanted to smooth that knot with my thumb. While at it, I could cup her face, run my fingers over her red lips, lean into her, inhale her sweet rose scent, and ki—

Why the fuck was I thinking about that now? I had been trying to banish her from my mind for two months. Winter break had been the worse, but I had succeeded. I hadn't gone to her. Now, she was right next to me. But it didn't matter. Why couldn't I keep control of my thoughts?

It wasn't my thoughts I couldn't control, though. It was my

heart. My emotions. I felt too much for this girl, and she could never know.

Finally, we arrived at the entrance of a cave at the base of the mountain.

"It's here," I said, gesturing to the cavern. "The mouth of the cave is the portal."

Erin halted by my side and stared at the vacant space in the surrounding stone. "Are you sure?"

I understood her skepticism. It looked like a normal cave with no markings, nothing different to tell this was a special, magical, and dangerous place.

"I am." It had been here where Asmodeus had called me to and taken me to the cemetery last November. I couldn't forget this place even if I tried.

"So, what do you need to do?" Claire gestured to her bag. "I've brought books on demonic spells, just in case."

A smile tugged at my lips, but I stopped myself. I could see why Erin liked Claire so much. She was good and kind and simple—not simple-minded, but simple to be around, simple to deal with. Easy. There was no drama, no rivalry, no attention seeking. And she was always prepared; it didn't matter what came their way.

"I don't think we'll need those this time," I said. I looked at Erin. "All we need to do is activate the portal, then close it."

Erin's brows curled down. "And how exactly do I close a portal?"

"Imagine it's a physical door and that you can shape it with your magic. With your hands." I waved my arm in front of us and a black sheen of darkfire, the size of a door, appeared in the snow. "Like this." I extended my arms, and with my hands shaped like claws, I molded the door to my will. Because I had conjured the door, it was easy to roll it up into a small ball. "The portal won't be this easy, but you get the gist."

"I see," she muttered.

"Are you ready?"

"You're going to activate the portal?"

I nodded. "Yup."

She let out a long breath and rolled her shoulders. "I'm ready."

I glanced at Claire. "You might want to stand back a bit, just in case."

Hugging her bag, Claire took several steps back and watched us.

A little wary, I walked closer to the cave's mouth. I cast a small sphere of darkfire in my hand and threw it right in the middle of the opening. The darkfire hit an invisible wall and dissipated in several rays. Then, the door appeared—an ancient stone arch framed the cave's mouth, with demonic runes carved on it. Its power flared, brushing against me and making the hair on my arms stand on end.

"Erin, watch out!" I cried as a demon burst through the portal and ran past me in a blur.

It was a screinor—a demon with long dark gray body, slicked with goo, a big mouth in a round head, and no visible eyes or ears. Their strike was strong, but their scream was the real weapon. When they shrieked, they disabled their victim.

Thankfully, Erin knew this. She shot the demon with a darkfire bolt as the demon opened its mouth. The demon deflected the hit, but it was distracted for a second. Meanwhile, Erin glanced to Claire. "Your Dawnblade!"

With shaking hands, Claire dropped her books and

summoned her sword. She ran and handed it to Erin as the demon skid to a stop a couple of feet from them and opened its huge mouth again.

My power thrumming inside my veins, I was about to shoot that fucking demon, but Erin swiped the sword wide and cut the demon's head off.

I stared at the demon's body and head lying in the snow, a little impressed with her. Apparently, she had not only been training in hand combat with Professor Martha, but also swordsmanship.

She nudged her chin at me. "That was it? Can we close it now?"

"Yes—" Two more screinors made it out of the portal. "Fuck."

I extended my hand and my Dawnblade appeared. I jumped out of the way of the screinors and cut them down before they got too close to Erin. Were they running straight at her because of the mark? Was it calling them? Or did they know who she was?

"Do it now," Claire urge. "Quick, before more come out!"

The Dawnblade disappeared from my hand and I faced the portal. A moment later, Erin was by my side.

"So, just imagine it's a door and mold it with my hands?"

"Right." I nodded once. "Let's do it."

I felt her power come forward, rubbing against me as it traveled to the portal. Following her lead, I channeled my magic again and enveloped the portal with it. I imagined it was fabric covering the cave's mouth. I needed to fold it up in my arms and put it away.

But it wasn't as easy as it looked. Even with Erin's powers added to mine, we still barely tickled the portal.

I wondered ...

I reached for her hand and entwined my fingers on hers. I felt her magic fade as she glanced at me with wide eyes. "What are you doing?"

"Uniting our magic."

She frowned at me. I closed my eyes for a moment and just felt it. We had a connection. We shared twin souls, which meant our magic was also compatible. We could act as one. So, I coaxed her magic, calling it into me.

Her magic didn't hesitate or protested. It jumped into me as if I was an extension of her, and obeyed my every wish. I sent our combined magic to the portal, and in no time, I saw the difference.

The stone arch shook, fighting against us.

Realizing what was happening, Erin stepped closer to me, her body pressed against mine, and rested her other hand over our joined ones. More of her power flowed into me.

She was so fucking powerful.

I threw all I had at the portal. The stone arch crumbled to the ground. Dark shadows rose from the broken pieces, swirling out of the snow and into the frigid air.

"It's done," I whispered, amazed with our work.

As if realizing she was touching me, Erin dropped her hands and took a large step back. "Right. We did it." She turned her back to me. "We should go now."

I stared at the broken portal. After we unified our magic, it had been so easy. Almost too easy.

"What is it?" Claire asked. She approached me. "Is something wrong?"

"I don't know," I said. "I thought it would be harder."

"Three demons came out of it, and we had to join forces to do it," Erin said, her tone curt again. "It was hard."

I didn't want to argue with her right now. I let the subject drop and guided them back to the academy. Because I didn't know how long our task would take, I scheduled the next hole in the guard patrol for later. We sought shelter under a curved tree trunk and waited.

With magic, I cleared some of the snow around the tree, so we could be less miserable in the cold than we already were.

Erin and Claire leaned against the tree trunk, and I stayed a couple of feet from them, watching for the patrol that was supposed to walk past the outpost soon.

Eyes closed, Claire held on to her bag, as if she was afraid of losing her books. Erin's brows were knotted, and she stared at her shaking hands.

I reached for her and enveloped her hands in mine. "Are you cold?"

She lifted her face, her eyes, somehow even more bright here in the near dark, found mine. "No." She pulled her hands from mine, and hid them behind her back.

Fuck, I had just touched her after being an ass to her. I couldn't blame her if she was confused after so many mixed signals. "What is it, then?"

She held my stare, but didn't say anything for a moment. When I had given up on an answer, she said, "Besides that general we killed together, this was the first time I killed someone."

"Not someone, a demon," I corrected her.

"I know, but killing is still killing." Her frown deepened. "I know that as a demon hunter I have to kill, and that demons are evil, but I hate being a killer."

"You can't think like that," Claire said. "I mean, I'm not one to be saying this. I won't become a full-fledged demon hunter, and hopefully, I won't have to kill any demons with my own hands, but you can't think of yourself as a killer. You're not killing an innocent person. You're killing a monster who will kill innocent people. Your work as a demon hunter is an honorable one."

"She's right." I was glad Claire had intervened, because if she hadn't, I wouldn't have been able to control my emotions. Right now, all I wanted was to reach over again and hug Erin. "You have to think of it as a service to the world."

"I know," she whispered. "I know."

Claire continued telling her about the big names in the demon hunter world. Randall was the most famous one by a mile, but there had been others who killed so many demons, or faced higher ones and didn't die, who had become legends. These hunters had doubts and families and lives like most of us, but they kept going, because their job was important.

Finally, the time came. "Two minutes until our window."

We waited and crossed through the gate without any problems.

When we were walking past the Daffodil building, Claire turned to us. "I need to ... hm, just go. Good night." She spun around and ran toward the Gardenia building alone.

"Claire!" Erin half-whispered. She turned to me, her cheeks so pink, I could see it even under the cover of night. "I don't know why she did that." She started walking faster. "I'll go see what happened."

"Erin," I called. She instantly slowed down again. "I insist on taking you to the dorms." Her eyes widened. Fuck, she would misinterpret this. "I mean, taking both of you, but since one ran off, I'll take you. I just want to make sure you two are delivered safely."

That was true, but I also had selfish intentions. I wanted

to enjoy her company for just a little longer. After, I would distance myself from her again.

Her brows knotted. "Of course."

Side by side, we walked past the Snapdragon building to the Gardenia building. I halted before the front steps.

Erin took a step forward, then stopped and faced me. She didn't say anything at first, but stared at me, with those big, beautiful golden eyes.

Why did she torture me like that? She had to know I was holding on by a thin thread right now, a thread that would break if she didn't walk away from me. If she didn't stop looking at me that way.

And then all my plans and my resolution would vanish, because I would kiss her with all I had.

"You think closing the portal will keep the demons away?" Her voice was a soft whisper.

This question was loaded. Yes, our first intention had been to close the fucking portal to keep everyone safe. But that wasn't the case anymore. I wanted to close it now to keep her safe. I knew it wouldn't stop the demons from coming after her, but it would make it harder.

"I hope it will," I said honestly.

She nodded. "Me too." She started up the stairs.

The word was out of my mouth before I could stop it. "Erin." She stopped and glanced at me again. I forced myself to continue, "Don't worry. Nothing will happen to you." Because I wouldn't let anything happen to her.

She nodded again, then went on. And I stayed frozen in the same spot, watching as Erin walked into the building, taking half of my heart with her.

I was glad she didn't look back at me before she disappeared inside the building—but I was also disappointed.

In need of a cold shower and an even colder beer, I headed back to my room.

5

ERIN

I WAS TIRED DURING MY TRAINING WITH MY MOTHER THE NEXT morning—I only got a few hours of sleep. I seriously had to stop with these late-night outings—but thankfully she didn't ask anything, and I didn't have to lie about my missions for Randall or sneaking out to close demonic portals.

After training, I went back to the dorm for breakfast, but I didn't change since my first class of the morning was martial arts. On my way to class, I saw Rey in the distance, walking from the Snapdragon building to the Orchid one.

My feelings for Rey had only grown, but when I got mad at him, I tried holding on to the feeling of rage, hoping it would erase the fondness in my heart.

I hated this hot and cold thing. He kept playing with me like a yo-yo. First, he cut me off, then he came after me. He held my hand, he asked me if I was okay, he stared at me, he told me he wanted to make sure I was safe ... When he stopped me last night, before I entered the dorms, I was sure he would give in, that he would tell me the truth, that he liked me too. And then he would kiss me.

Apparently, that was all in my dreams.

This semester, Claire wasn't in my martial arts class again. But Ava and her friends, Stella and Ruby, were.

After telling the class that we would be moving on to specific weapons this semester, and showing us some basic moves with a bo staff to start with—overhead strike, four-point strike, front thrust, and a few others—professor Genevieve separated the class into pairs. "Erin, Ava, you're partners."

I stared at Ava. Really? Again? At least this time I wouldn't get my ass kicked so easily.

Ava and I grabbed bo staffs from the cart Professor Genevieve had brought over, and we faced each other in a corner of the mat.

As usual, Ava couldn't hide her feelings. With rage stamped in her eyes, she advanced toward me. She did a front thrust, reaching far. I sidestepped to the right, and did an overhead strike. While her bo staff only grazed my arm, I hit her hard in the shoulder before she moved away.

That only sparked more anger from her.

"You're so full of yourself," she snapped.

"Me?" I snorted. "You're the one who thinks you're the queen of the academy."

She came at me, swiping the bo staff left and right, without any clear technique, but eager to strike me. I stepped back, but because of the limited space with the other students practicing at the same time, I had nowhere to go. I ducked under her staff, trying to spin around and away, but she let the bo staff fall on my back.

Pain exploded through my muscles, radiating down my lower back.

"You bitch," I snarled between gritted teeth.

"Me? You're the one with tainted blood." She showed me a wicked grin before striking again.

I rolled back and jumped up. Anything to get away from another hit like that. But she didn't relent, and I wasn't going to back down either.

Pissed off, I lunged at her with a spinning strike, then an uppercut strike. She barely had time to raise her bow and block my hit from landing on her chin. The force of the impact jarred her, though, and she stumbled back.

Once more, that only ignited more of her spite.

"I'm going to kill you," Ava said with a grunt. She spun the bo staff as if she would strike me on my left side, but then she stepped back and hit me with the tip of the staff in my ribs.

I gasped as the air fled from my lungs and a burning pain spread through my chest.

Without giving me time to breathe, Ava was on me again. We exchanged a series of strikes. Most of the time, we were able to block or get away before the hit landed, but sometimes ... sometimes the bo staff met its mark and it hurt like hell.

Ava brought her knee up, with the bo staff over her shoulder. Anticipating an overhead strike, I raised my bo staff to block her hit, then did a quick four-point strike, hitting her shoulders and the sides of her ribs. She let out an exasperated grunt, probably in pain.

It served her right.

Even with my back and my chest screaming at me, I positioned myself to continue our fight.

A bo staff appeared over mine, pushing it to the ground. "Enough!" Professor Genevieve snapped. "Unless you want to be suspended, stop it now!"

I stared at her, at her bo staff blocking mine from hitting Ava, at Ava's hateful glare, at my anger.

Ashamed of myself for allowing Ava to drag me so low, I dropped the staff. It clanked on the mat and rolled away.

Ava hesitated, but she too lowered her weapon and took a step back.

Around us, the entire class was frozen, everyone's eyes on us.

"I don't even want to talk to you two now." Professor Genevieve pointed to the door. "Get out before I fail you both."

I picked up my staff from the mat and put it on the cart in the middle of the classroom, then I marched out, trying not to let the stares and whispers get to me.

When I got outside the Hyacinth building, the chilly wind whipped around me, and the throbbing pain in my chest instantly got better. Shit, Ava and I had gone too far. I glanced down at myself—my chest and arms were covered with my combat uniform, but I bet I had at least five ugly bruises where she struck me. I bet she had just as many.

Before I got too cold, I ran back to the dorms, where I holed up in my bedroom, took a nice warm shower, and applied some healing cream to my bruises. I got dressed in the academy's uniform, put on my heavy coat on top of that, took some medicine for pain, and headed to the cafeteria to meet Claire for lunch.

Claire was already at our usual small round table by the glass walls, her elbow on the top and her chin on her hand. Her green eyes stared out at the sky, a smile on her lips, as if she was seeing a rainbow instead of the ugly gray day.

"What's up with you?" I asked, taking a seat beside her.

She let out a sigh. "I—"

"Hi."

I turned to the new voice and saw a guy standing beside me. "Hm, hi."

He extended his hand at me. "I'm Tanner. I'm a third-year student."

I frowned, trying to remember him from around campus, but it didn't ring a bell. Which didn't mean much. I still didn't know everyone who studied here, but I couldn't deny he was handsome. He was tall and wide, with brown curls, and smooth tanned skin. If I had seen him before, I would have certainly remembered.

I took his hand. "Erin."

"I know." He sat down beside Claire. I stared at my friend, but Claire was staring at Tanner. "I was just talking to Claire about you."

I took a seat across the table. "Really? What about?"

"Nothing much." He faced Claire, his eyes locked on hers. "How you're a good friend to her, and how you stand by her side no matter what." Claire practically swooned.

"Oh-kay," I dragged out. What was going on?

Tanner looked at me, his eyes on my neck. "What happened?"

I touched my neck. One of the bruises on my shoulder had a big purple mark and it showed on my neck. "I was fighting Ava."

"Ow, that must hurt." Tanner patted Claire's hand. "I'll let you take care of your friend, then. See you later."

He stood and walked away. I watched as he went to the other side of the cafeteria and sat down with the other guys from the third year.

In a flash, Claire switched seats and pressed to my side. "So, what did you think?"

"About?" I asked, lost.

"Tanner." She let out a long sigh. "Isn't he gorgeous? Isn't he sweet? Holy crap, he's perfect."

I frowned. It was hard for me to look at any other guy like that. I liked Rey, even if he wasn't my supposed soulmate. "If you say so."

"If I was a little braver, I would ask him out on a date," Claire said.

"How can one go out on a date when we aren't supposed to leave campus?" I asked, curious about it.

"Well, there's the cafeteria, the media room, the library. Also, haven't you heard about the movie room? I heard it's changing location this semester, but it should be up and running soon." She wiggled her eyebrows at me. "That is a perfect place for a date."

"You like Tanner?" I asked, still confused. "How did this happen?"

"He walked with me from my previous class. He even carried my bookbag." She swooned again. "He's perfect."

"You've already said that."

"I know, but he is."

"Okay, okay." I patted her shoulder, trying to calm her down. I didn't see the big deal about Tanner, and I honestly didn't like the way he talked to me and looked at her, but Claire seemed so happy about the attention, I decided to leave it. For now. "I'm hungry." I got up. "Let's eat."

We both headed toward the buffet at the back of the cafeteria, where we got our lunch, and went back to our table. Despite myself, I kept glancing around, searching for Rey, but I didn't know why. He rarely ate in the cafeteria. Instead, I got a glimpse of Harvey and Peter, who waved at me; Ava, with a red bruise on her chin, and her dear friends, Stella and Ruby;

and Harper, who was sitting alone at a table along the farthest wall.

I frowned, thinking of how she had lost her two best friends recently. Now she was alone and seemed way too pitiful.

A sudden urge to go check on her hit me hard, but before I could act on it, the amulet around my neck shone—a dark light that seemed to come from inside.

"What's that?" Claire asked, pointing to it. "Why is it shining?"

"It's nothing." I put the necklace under my sweater, and looked around.

This was it. A warning. Someone in here was a half-demon, like me.

My eyes found a young man leaving the cafeteria and the amulet shook against me.

It was a warning.

I had found the first half-demon.

6

REY

ONE OF THE THINGS RANDALL ASKED OF ME AFTER MAKING OUR deal was for me to take my classes seriously. I wasn't pretending to be a demon hunter anymore. He planned on making me a real one. And he wanted me to be a professor after graduation, so I could still be under his thumb, I was sure.

How he would make me into a real demon hunter, I had no idea, and right now, I didn't really want to know. As long as I got to stay here and watch over Erin, I was okay with it.

So, I went to my classes, paid attention, and decided it was time to get even better grades than my current great ones. I would amaze all my professors and they would all vouch for me.

I left my last class of the day with a sense of a job well done.

But that all vanished when I saw Erin coming my way.

Hadn't I told her to stay the fuck away from me? Hadn't I been rude enough? Hadn't I made myself clear? I didn't want to hurt her anymore.

Out in the cold, Erin halted in front of me. "I need to talk to you."

"I have nothing to talk to you about," I said, walking around her.

Her hand shot out and grabbed my arm. "Stop being a jerk and listen to me. The amulet gave me a warning. I saw a half-demon on campus."

All right. That was important, but I freed my arm from her grip before asking, "Who is it?"

"I don't know. I tried to follow him, but I lost him around lunchtime. I've been searching for him ever since, but I can't find him. He's average height, with blond hair to his chin, and I think he's your age." She paused. "I mean, your human age."

I thought for a moment. My age meant this guy was in the fourth year. An average guy with blond hair to his chin? It could only be ... "Zachary."

"Do you know his room number?"

"He doesn't live on campus anymore."

Erin frowned. "What do you mean?"

"He got married and was given permission to live in Chasseur Ville with his wife."

"I wasn't even sure that was allowed," she muttered. "Anyway, do you think he has any classes now? If not, we should go after him."

"Right now?" I checked my wristwatch. It was four in the evening. Being winter, and with a gray day like today, that meant that it would be pitch black in about an hour.

"Do you have a better idea?" she asked, her tone a little harsher. "It's either go now, or tomorrow during class time."

I groaned. "You're right."

Together, we stopped by the archives and found out Zachary's last class of the day had been that afternoon, which meant he had already left for the village. I copied his exact address from his file, before we went to the underground garage, where we got my car and left the academy. I had always had permission to come and go from the academy whenever I wanted, but now Erin had it too—but only Randall's permission.

We remained silent as I drove to Chasseur Ville, but my fucking mind didn't stop.

My plan wasn't working. Wanting to stay away from Erin, and staying away from Erin were proving to be different things. If I wanted not to get any more involved with her than I already had, I needed a new plan.

But what? What could I do to keep her away from me?

I sometimes wondered if that was fucking possible. With her being my twin soul, I doubted I could stay away forever.

I glanced at her. She was looking straight ahead, serious. The darkening sky gave her pretty face a deep shadow. And then I saw it, the dark shadow on her neck.

"What the fuck is that?"

Erin turned wide eyes to me. "What?"

"That bruise on your neck?"

"Oh." She covered the bruise with her hand. "It's nothing."

"The fuck it's nothing." Rage filled my chest. If someone hurt her on purpose … "Tell me."

"Why?" she snapped, staring daggers at me. "Why do I have to tell you? You've made it clear that you don't care what happens to me. All that matters is getting this damn job done, so focus on the freaking road and forget about me."

Her words … they hurt. I grabbed the steering wheel until my knuckles turned white. I was even more curious now.

What the fuck could have happened for her to have that bruise? What was she hiding?

On the other hand, it was working. She had just been mean to me to fend me off. I had to hang on a little more. Soon, I would be able to resist her completely, and she would forget about me.

It was full night when we arrived in Chasseur Ville. Even with the fucking cold and the threat of more snow, the tourists were showing up for the night.

"Does this town ever stop?" Erin asked as we drove down the main road.

"Not really," I said, looking around. "On a night like this, it might slow down a bit, but it never stops."

I drove past the castle, to the quieter part of town, where most of the former demon hunter's residences were. We followed the address in the academy's archive to a small chalet, the last one on a quiet street.

I parked my car at the property's entrance and hopped out. The long driveway had been shoveled, but there was still plenty of ice covering it. I felt the urge to hold Erin's arm, but kept my hands to myself. Hadn't I just realized she was making progress? I couldn't taint it now.

Together, we walked down the driveaway and knocked on the front door.

A moment later, Zachary opened the door. "Rey? Erin? What are you two doing here?"

I frowned. He knew Erin? Well, not even five months ago, she had been the new girl on campus. Probably everyone at the academy knew her name.

"We need to talk to you," I told him.

Zachary crossed his arms. "About?"

"The truth about your bloodline."

His brown eyes went wide. "What the hell?" He stepped out the door and closed it. "What are you talking about?"

"By your reaction, I'd say you know what we're talking about," Erin said.

"No, I don't," Zachary said, his tone unsure.

"If you need me to spell it out, I will," I told him. "You're a half-demon, just like Erin and me."

Zachary glanced around, obviously freaked out. "Keep it down, will you? I don't want anyone around here to know."

"So you're not denying it," Erin observed.

"I doubt denying would change anything." Zachary shook his head. "It's not like I can change it, but if I had a choice, I would be a normal hunter, no demon blood in my veins."

"We know how you feel," Erin said, her tone low. Sad.

"You know the truth," Zachary said, still on the defensive. "Now what the hell do you want?"

"Headmaster Randall wants to create a unit of half-demons, so in time, we can erase the prejudice and have a more inclusive hunter academy," I told him. "Randall would like you to join the Black Knight Unit."

Zachary shook his head. "That's insane. I don't want to be a half-demon, and I don't want to join other half-demons in anything."

"Zachary, listen to us—"

A darkfire bolt appeared in Zachary's hand. "I'm going to say it just this once. Go away and forget about me."

Erin lifted her hands. "We're not here to—"

Zachary threw the bolt at her.

My rage spiked and I brought up a shield in front of Erin. The bolt exploded against my shield, both darkfires fading away in the dark.

I conjured darkfire that enveloped both my hands and faced the guy. "Try that again and you're dead."

"Zack? What's happening?"

Zachary's face blanched at the new voice. "That's my wife," he whispered in a rush. "She doesn't know I'm a half-demon." He waved at my hands. "Drop the damn magic!"

I let go and the darkfire faded like smoke in the wind.

A second later, the front door opened and Susan stared at us. "Oh, hello." She glanced at her husband. "What's going on?"

"Hey, baby, these are my friends from school," Zachary said. His wife was of demon hunter lineage, but her parents had opted not to send her to the academy—which was rare. Instead, she worked at her parents' store in Chasseur Ville.

Erin lifted her hand and wiggled her fingers. "Hi."

"It's cold outside," Susan said. "Do you guys want to come in?"

"No, it's fine," I said, my voice plain. "We just came to discuss something about a project and will be leaving soon."

"You can go back inside, baby," Zachary said, with an uneasy smile. "I'll be right there."

"Okay." Frowning, Susan turned and closed the door behind her.

"Please, just get out of here before she finds out," Zachary urged.

This was my opportunity. The deal-dealing son of Asmodeus came out. "We won't tell her anything if you join the Black Knight Unit."

Erin turned her big eyes to me.

Zachary cursed under his breath. "Fine!"

I extended my hand to Erin and she handed me an

amulet, just like the one she was wearing. "Wear this. When we need you, the amulet will let you know."

Reluctantly, Zachary grabbed the amulet and put it around his neck. "Happy? Now leave." He entered his house and slammed the door in our faces.

Without a second to spare, Erin marched back to my car. She hopped in, put on her seat belt, and crossed her arms. I could see—feel—something was bothering.

I didn't want to pretend I didn't know.

"Are you going to huff and puff until we get to the academy?" I asked as I drove away from Chasseur Ville.

She turned her glare to me. "You blackmailed him."

I nodded. "Yes, I did."

"I know that's what you used to do for Asmodeus, but you don't need to do it anymore."

"It went well. He just needed a little motivation."

"Would you have told his wife if he had said no?"

I didn't answer right away, because I really didn't know what I would have done. "He said yes; that's all that matters."

"I really don't like this," she muttered.

"Look, if we can't get half-demons to join us, Randall will expose you and punish me. I did what I had to do."

"You say that as if the headmaster is a bad guy."

I pressed my lips together. I didn't want to shatter the vision that she had that Randall was like a god, and the academy was the best place in the world. After all, I had been the one to bring her to this fucking place. Now, she was stuck here, practically a prisoner of the man who was supposed to be the reason and truth among us all.

"Our unit is growing, that's all that matters," I repeated, not happy with myself either.

"I don't know what's going on," she said, her voice low. "I

don't know if you were always like this and only changed after what happened in the cemetery, or if you're just changing now. But I'm not sure I like this cold, harsh Rey."

"Good," I snapped. "You're not supposed to like me anyway."

Erin's mouth fell open. A moment later, she forced it shut and stared straight ahead, her back glued to the passenger seat. She didn't say anything else during the rest of the ride, and once I parked the car in the underground garage, she was out the door in a flash.

She didn't say good night, wave at me, or glance back as she stomped back to her dorm.

But I followed her. I watched her. I wanted to make sure she got to her bedroom safe. Once the light in her bedroom window shone from the second floor, I let out a long breath and dragged my feet to my room.

All I had to do was to be a jerk. If I kept this up, she would move on soon.

But I doubted I would.

7

ERIN

THE FIRST WEEK BACK AT THE ACADEMY WENT BY TOO FAST. After my fight with Ava, and finding out about Zachary, nothing else happened. In the next martial arts class, Ava and I avoided each other despite being partners, my amulet didn't warn me of any new sightings, the headmaster hadn't sent for me, and I had barely seen Rey around.

Rey, the jerk.

I still couldn't figure him out. At first, I thought he was being a jerk and pushing me away, but now I was starting to doubt it. Perhaps he had always been a douche, but he had played me to find out about my half-demon side. The way he blackmailed Zachary last week? I really didn't like it.

And the way he hadn't answered me when I mentioned the headmaster was a bad guy ... what did that mean? Was the headmaster a bad guy? But he couldn't be. He had been given these amazing powers, and founded the Blackthorn Hunters and the academy to save the world from evil. Plus, he had saved Rey's life and was protecting me from bigger threats.

If the headmaster said he wanted to help half-demons and introduce them to the hunter society, I chose to believe him. Because that was exactly what I wanted to happen.

In the middle of the second week back, I went to potion-making class and took my place beside Claire, but Professor Wesley rearranged our seats and I was partnered with Harvey.

"Hello, beautiful," he said, taking the seat beside mine. The young man with brown hair and warm chocolate eyes offered me a half-smile. If this were a regular high school or college, Harvey Walton would be like the football team's quarterback. Hot, dreamy, and way too flirty with all the girls. "Have you been avoiding me?"

I chuckled. "No, I haven't. Maybe Ava is hogging all of your time."

He rolled his eyes. "Let's not talk about her."

I glanced to where Ava was, a couple of tables in front of us, with Harper as a partner. Poor Harper had to endure Ava's mood swings for the rest of the semester. "Why not? It's obvious that she thinks you two are practically engaged."

"I know." He let out a sigh. "But seriously, I really don't want to talk about her." He leaned over the table, his head on his hand, and stared at me. "I would rather talk about you."

"You know what I am," I whispered. Harvey had been present last semester when Asmodeus had told us about my heritage. "And you still want to talk to me?"

"It doesn't matter what you are. All that matters is that you're interesting."

I ignored him and opened my potions book to chapter nine. Today, we would work on a healing potion used by witches. It was said to be simple, but effective for minor injuries. For some reason, I wanted to ace this potion.

I started reading through the chapter, and Harvey kept staring at me. What the hell? Wasn't he going to help me? Or was he planning on staring at me all semester? Hm, was he playing around? I remembered Claire telling me Harvey didn't flirt long with the same girl; he moved on quickly. However, from what I could gather, he had been flirting with me for the last five months.

And I hadn't seen him with any other girl on campus during that time. Unless, he met them in secret. But I doubted things like that stayed quiet for long here.

Could it be ...?

I lifted my gaze to Harvey. His smile widened. All right, okay, he was handsome; I had already noticed that. He came from a good family, and he seemed to be into me.

Would it be hard to consider this? He and I?

This was nonsense. I didn't have time for this. If I went out with Harvey, it would be because I was trying to nurse my broken heart. I was fine by myself. No men needed.

I placed a hand on my chest, where the soul bond mark was.

Shit, I was fine by myself, but apparently, someone was looking for me.

Shaking my head, I went to the pantry in the back of the classroom, and grabbed the potion ingredients. I spread them out on the table and started sorting them, ensuring I had everything we needed.

"Just to let you know, I suck at this," I told Harvey, who was still staring at me like a starstruck boy. "This class was my lowest grade last semester. If you don't help me, you'll get a low grade too." I doubted his mother, Professor Eleanor, would like that.

"Let's go on a date," he said suddenly.

I almost dropped the vial I was holding. "What?"

"Let's go on a date," he repeated, straightening up, though his eyes stayed glued to me. "Tonight. Let me take you to a restaurant on a date."

I frowned. "Students aren't allowed outside the academy during the semester." Although the headmaster had allowed me to leave, when I had a mission outside. This wasn't the case.

"For most things, no, they aren't," he said. "But I have my ways. Leave it to me. I can get both of us out of the academy tonight."

I raised my eyebrows at him. "Are you talking about sneaking out?" I had my fair share of sneaking out already, and I sure didn't want to do that anymore.

"No, I think I can manage to do it with authorization," he said. How? Would he ask his mother to let us out? She would never allow him to go out with me. "So?"

I stared at him some more. He was handsome, he was nice to me, and he was available. Why not? What was the worst that could happen? To find out he wasn't the one for me, or the one marked on my skin.

I nodded. "All right. Let's go out on a date."

* * *

OF COURSE, AVA FOUND OUT ABOUT IT IN FIVE SECONDS FLAT. She pursued me after class and demanded an explanation. I would have been the best woman if I had kept quiet and walked away, but I liked seeing her miserable—and I hated that about me.

So, I goaded her, saying yes, I was going on a date with

Harvey. "Excuse me, I have to find some proper, sexy clothes for tonight," I told her before walking away.

She was fuming, but Stella and Ruby stopped her from lunging at me.

I knew that had been petty of me, but I couldn't help it. Ava was a bitch and I wish I could teach her a lesson. If this was it, then so be it.

After the day's classes were done, Claire met me in my room and we went through my closet.

"I can't believe you're going out with Harvey," Claire said. She picked up a black blouse, put it in front of herself, and looked at the mirror.

"Me neither," I said, shaking my head. That blouse was too plain. "How about this one?" I placed an off-shoulder red blouse with long sleeves in front of me.

"Oh, I like that." She started rummaging through my closet again. "Please, tell me you have a pair of tight, sexy leather leggings to go with it?"

"As a matter of fact ..." I opened the second drawer of my dresser and pulled out said pants. I had bought them a couple of years ago on a whim and never wore them.

"Holy crap, now all you need is a pair of killer stiletto boots."

Harper, who was walking past my half-open door, knocked once and stuck her head inside. "Someone say killer stiletto boots? I might be able to help with that."

Turned out, Harper had the perfect boots to go with the pants. Like me and my pants, she said she had fallen in love with them, but never wore them. She lent them to me with a smile on her face.

"Thanks so much," I said, smiling back.

"My pleasure," she replied.

It was good to see her in good spirits for once, so I invited her to stay in my room while I finished getting ready. In the end, it was a good thing, because Harper was good with makeup too. "Another thing I picked up that is practically useless here," she said as she worked on making sexy, smoky eyes on me.

"Well, there's no school rule saying you can't wear makeup to class," Claire said.

"Have you seen Ava and her troupe?" I asked. "They're always wearing a lot of makeup."

Harper chuckled. "True. I do wear makeup, but it's too neutral to be noticeable." She handed me a red lipstick and let me apply that. "You were already beautiful to start with, now you're stunning."

I smiled wide. "Thanks." But my smile died a second later. Why was I putting so much effort in dressing up and getting beautified for Harvey? I wasn't into him. Unless, he changed my heart tonight, which honestly, I wouldn't mind happening.

Or perhaps ... I had dressed up hoping Rey would see me. Maybe he would find me before I left the grounds, and he would see how sexy and gorgeous I was. Maybe it would get to him and mess with his mind, and he wouldn't be able to resist telling me how he really felt about me. Then, he would whisk me away and kiss me senseless.

Sigh. Only in my dreams.

I combed my hair back until it was straight like a board and shining, put on my wool-lined leather jacket, and went downstairs to meet Harvey. He was waiting for me in the lobby, wearing casual pants, a nice sweater, and a suede jacket. His brown hair was combed back, showing off his handsome face.

When he saw me, his eyes went wide. "Holy shit," he muttered. "You look … amazing."

I smiled, feeling good about this. After suffering for so long and agonizing over my uncertain future, I thought I deserved this feeling and embraced it. Even if it was for one night, I wanted to enjoy the dinner, the company, the production.

"You did it," I said, a little stunned we were leaving campus. I didn't want to admit it, but there were moments I had doubted he would pull this off. "How did you do it?"

He grinned at me. "I asked your mother."

I glanced around, but there was no one nearby to hear him. Though Harvey knew Professor Martha was my mother, we weren't advertising it. "How?"

"I told her I wanted to take her daughter out on a date," he said. "Perhaps she thinks I'm a good catch." He winked at me.

Suppressing a chuckle, I rolled my eyes at him.

Harvey took my arm and helped me down the snow-flanked paths to the underground garage. I couldn't help but notice that even though I was wearing five-inch heels, Harvey was still half a head taller than me—which was always nice.

In the garage, my eyes won and I ended up glancing at Rey's usual spot. His car was there, which meant he was at the academy.

And he hadn't seen me like I had hoped he would.

"Here." Harvey opened the passenger door of a big, fancy SUV for me.

"Whose car is this?" I asked as I entered the car.

Harvey closed my door, and went to the other side, where he sat behind the steering wheel. Only then did he answer, "Mine."

I frowned. "Students have their own cars?"

He shook his head. "No. Actually most students can't have cars, only a few." He glanced at me. "You know who my mother and father are. Usually, I hate when they pull strings for me, but this time, I didn't mind."

Harvey turned on the engine, and drove out of the garage. He had to stop at the main gates and show the guards the pass from my mother—a similar one I had, but mine was for walking around campus late at night. Harvey's was for permission to leave the academy with me for tonight only.

"Stay safe," the guard told us.

"We will," Harvey replied before peeling away.

He drove us to West Hill, a small town near the academy. There, he took us to a fancy Italian restaurant.

"Reservation for Harvey Walton," he said to the hostess once we walked into the restaurant.

I stared at him, a little surprised. He had even called ahead and made a reservation. Wow.

"Right this way, please," the hostess said. She took us to a large, round booth in the corner of the restaurant. "Your server will be right with you. Enjoy your dinner."

"Thank you," I muttered, starting to think this wasn't a good idea after all.

Harvey had dressed up, he had asked my mother's permission, and he had made reservations at this expensive restaurant—from the looks of it. I had dressed up too, and now that we were here alone, it felt somewhat wrong.

"Relax," Harvey said. He opened my menu for me. "I can see you're tense. Just relax. Try to enjoy the night without any pressure. I want you to have a good time even if by the end of the night you decide you prefer being only friends."

Shit, his damn words. Why couldn't I swoon and fall for him already? It would make my life so much easier.

Determined to have a good night, I heeded his words. When the waitress came back, we ordered our drinks and an appetizer. Then, Harvey launched into stories about himself —good ones. He told me when he and Peter sneaked into the academy, when they were still young and untrained, and managed to attend three classes before they were caught. Another time, they sneaked into the full-fledged Blackthorn Hunters outpost a few miles up the mountain from the academy. They saw the hunters bring a higher demon into the compound, detain it, and interrogate it. They were discovered, though, and grounded for an entire year.

Not long ago, Harvey had been good friends with Rey too. Did he have any stories about him? Would he tell me? I didn't want to bring up Rey when the night was going so well, but I couldn't shut down my brain, even if I tried. Rey was always on my mind, as was the soul bond mark and the fact that I thought Harvey wasn't the one to bear one like mine. Several times urges to grab the collar of his sweater and pull it down hit me hard, but I held it in. If he was the one with the mark like mine, I was sure he would have already told me about it. Well, with his personality, he would have gone around campus, bragging about the mark and asking all the girls who his soulmate was.

In the end, I knew Harvey wasn't the one for me. He was handsome, he was fun, he was nice, but that was all. He was a friend I could count on—I knew that because he had helped me before. He knew my secret, he had fought alongside me, and he hadn't told anyone. He still flirted with me and hung around me as if I wasn't half a monster.

Harvey was a good friend, nothing more.

After the main entree and dessert, Harvey asked for the bill. I insisted on paying for my part, but he ignored me.

"I invited you, so it's my treat," he said, never losing that easygoing half-grin. He handed the credit card to the waitress.

"Be right back," she said, walking away with the card in hand.

Then, the front doors burst open and the entire building shook as a loud boom echoed through the place, and a rage of fire rolled inside.

8

AFTER CLASS, I HAD A MEETING WITH RANDALL. FOR THE MOST part, he left Erin out of his schemes, which I was grateful for, but that meant I had to meet the headmaster and report on our progress by myself. I told him about Zachary and how I persuaded him to join the Black Knight Unit.

"Good job," Randall said.

I should have been proud of myself for ripping a compliment from him, but I only felt disgusted with myself. If Erin felt like this about me, then I was certainly succeeding in pushing her away.

But I fucking hated this. I hated to think she was disgusted with me. Couldn't I be a jerk with a conscience?

Before I realized what I was doing, I entered the Gardenia building. I stopped myself in the lobby and shook my head. What the fuck was I doing? Going after Erin? Why? I couldn't try to mend things now. It would only send her more mixed signals.

I turned around to leave and almost bumped into Claire, who was walking in.

She frowned at me. "Rey? Are you looking for Erin? She isn't here."

That piqued my curiosity. "Where is she?"

Claire smiled at me. "She went on a date with Harvey."

I blinked, not sure I heard her right. "What?"

"It was really cute," Claire went on, oblivious to the jealousy and rage swimming within me. "He asked her out in the middle of class. Between us, I think he really likes her."

The question was, did she like him? I wanted to ask Claire, but I asked something else instead. "Where did they go?"

"West Hill, though I don't know which restaurant."

"Thanks." I dashed away, almost slipping on the front stairs. I ran into the underground garage, got my car, and drove to West Hill.

My brain wasn't functioning right now. All it thought about was Harvey leaning into Erin and kissing her. That sent a pang of fury through my veins, boiling my blood.

I needed to find them. I needed to stop them.

My rage subsided a little when I drove into town and found it in chaos. Humans ran down the streets, screaming, while Blackthorn Hunters in full battle gear stomped around town, searching for something.

I dropped my car in an empty parking lot and ran to the nearest demon hunter.

"Andre, what's going on?"

Andre, a tall, muscular black man in his early thirties with long dreadlocks turned to me. "Rey. What are you doing here?"

Because of my status with Randall, I knew all the demon hunters—the active ones, the retired ones, the ones who had died in battle—and they all knew me. Some hated me for being so young and so favored (they didn't know my real age, of course), while some were friendly.

Andre was a friendly one.

"I was coming to pick up something," I lied.

Another wave of humans ran past us.

"This way!" Like a traffic officer, Andre gestured to the humans to continued down the road, away from the downtown area.

"What's going on?" I asked again once the humans were gone.

"We're on a hunt," he said. "A dangerous fae was spotted in town. She blasted her frost powers at us and almost hit several civilians. We need to stop her before she escapes and hurts more people."

Unlike the demon hunters, I had had contact with several supernaturals, and one thing I knew for sure: not all of them were evil like the demon hunters professed. Wyatt was the first one to come to mind. He was a werewolf, and besides a few bouts of his rage spiking, he was as good as they came.

"I have friends from the academy in town," I told him. "I'll find them, then I'll join you."

"That would be great." The Dawnblade appeared in his hand. "Be careful," he said before running into an alley to search for the fae.

I ran closer to downtown, the scent of smoke reaching my nose. I spotted more Blackthorn Hunters and talked to them, but none had seen students from the academy around. I hadn't seen Hadrian, Harvey's father, around, but I was sure the other hunters knew who Harvey was. If they had seen him, they would have escorted him—and Erin—to safety.

Right around the green, businesses were destroyed and on fire. The demon hunters had called the firefighters, but they seemed skeptical about the big people in fancy black leather uniforms.

My chest constricted a little more with every step I took. Where the fuck was Erin? What had happened to her?

At the corner of the green, I spotted Norah exiting a store that had been burned to the ground.

"Rey, didn't expect to see you here," she said, halting before me. Norah was a recent graduate of the academy. Since she first entered the academy, she had been praised for being one of the best students, and comments about her bright future only increased as the years passed. As soon as she finished the fourth year, Norah joined the main demon hunter group and was well on her way to becoming a legend.

"I'm looking for my friends from the academy," I told her.

She frowned, her green eyes becoming two slits. "I haven't seen any students around."

"Well, if you do, hold on to them and call me." I patted my pocket. Though there was a rule that students couldn't carry their phones in the academy, there was no such rule for the full-fledged hunters.

"Will do," she said, before walking into the next store, also half-destroyed by the fire.

A frost fae that set fire to town? That didn't make sense.

Shaking my head, I moved on.

I was about to go crazy when I saw them. Erin and Harvey were seated on a wooden bench in the middle of the green. The first thing I noticed was how beautiful Erin looked—and sexy. She wore tight leather pants, tall heeled boots, and a red blouse that showed off her shoulders. Where the fuck was her coat?

She had dressed up like that to go out with Harvey. That knowledge fucking hurt.

The second thing I noticed was that Harvey was tying a piece of cloth around Erin's hand.

I stomped to them. "What the fuck?"

Harvey's hand froze. "Rey."

Erin turned big eyes to me. "What are you doing here?"

I shoved my finger into Harvey's face. "What the fuck were you thinking? Taking her out of the academy? Look what the fuck happened!"

Erin cradled her hurt hand. "This isn't his fault."

"Rey, chill out," Harvey said.

That only made me angrier.

Doreen, a female demon hunter with red hair and in her thirties, approached us. "What's going on here?"

"Nothing," I snapped. "I told Andre that I would help, but I think it's best if I escort these two back to the academy."

Doreen nodded. "Sounds like a good idea." She pointed to her back. "Take the south road. We already swept that area and found nothing. You all should be safe."

"Thanks, Doreen," I said.

Doreen narrowed her hazel eyes at Harvey. "Should I tell your father about this?"

Harvey grimaced. "Please, don't."

"Get out of here safe in the next few minutes and I won't." Doreen winked, then stalked away, in the direction of the other demon hunters.

Harvey stood up. He grabbed Erin's unhurt hand and tugged her up. I wanted to break all his fingers right now.

"What's going on?" Erin asked, her eyes on the group of demon hunters that ran past the green and disappeared down a side road.

"They are hunting a frost fae," I told them. "And I'm in charge of taking you both to the academy." I reached for Erin.

She took a step back. "You sound like you're a lot older than we are."

"Well, you two know I'm a lot older than anyone in this fucking town," I snapped.

"You know what I mean." She crossed her arms in defiance. "You're a student like us, not a professor or a full-fledged demon hunter."

"What the fuck?" I muttered. "You know my authority and you two are coming with me right now, or so help me." My rage spiked and darkfire enveloped my hands.

Gasping, Erin took another step back.

Harvey raised both hands in a sign of peace. "Dude, chill out."

Fuck. I let out a long breath and dropped my magic. "You heard Doreen. We have to go now, down the south road, or she'll tell your father, and probably your mother—" I was sure Professor Martha would be furious about this. "—about where you were when chaos hit West Hill."

Harvey cursed under his breath. "All right, let's go." He stomped past me, toward the south road.

Erin remained frozen for a few more seconds, shooting me daggers with her golden eyes. Finally, she let out a long, exasperated breath and followed Harvey. And I followed them both.

I tried calming down as we walked down the south road. If I got in my car with them feeling like this, I was certain to either drive into a tree, or punch Harvey.

Or both.

I inhaled deeply, holding the air for a few seconds, before letting it go. Holy fuck, so many things could have gone wrong tonight. Erin could have been hurt, Harvey too. Harvey's parents could have found them out—Harvey would have been grounded, and his parents would have shunned Erin, and because of their influence at the academy, others would follow their example.

And Erin would realize I had come after her. That I was dying of jealousy. That I wanted to tell Harvey to fuck off. That I wanted to grab Erin and kiss her.

Ever since seeing her on the bench without a coat, I wanted to take mine off and offer it to her, but once again, that would only send her mixed signals.

I let out another long breath.

A few feet in front of me, Erin halted. I slowed down and stopped by her side. "What is it?"

She glanced to a small townhouse on the left. "Look at the window."

I did. Faint white light shone from inside. It flickered as if magic was being used every few seconds.

I frowned. "The demon hunters said they swept this road."

"Maybe that's why the fae is back here," Erin said. "Because he knows the hunters won't come looking for him here."

"Her," I corrected her. "Andre told me it's a female." Eyes on the window, Erin took a step toward it. I snatched her arm. "What the fuck do you think you're doing?"

She halted, as if realizing what she had been about to do. "I don't know," she whispered. Then, she glanced up at me. "Is there a way you can contact the other hunters and let them know the fae is here?"

I reached for my phone inside my jacket, but I didn't have it with me. In my rush to come after her, I had left my phone in my room. "We can go back and let them know."

"I have another idea," Harvey said. I followed his voice and found him sneaking up to the townhouse.

"Harvey! What the fuck?"

Harvey put a finger over his lips. "We capture this fae and we'll be heroes!" He stalked closer to the house.

"We have to stop him," Erin said, going after him.

I ran past her, going directly to Harvey to stop him, but the little shit saw me coming and he sped up. Summoning his Dawnblade, he pushed in the front door and burst inside the house.

"No!" Erin screamed.

She and I entered the house together and froze at the door.

Inside, a young female fae cowered in the corner, a wound on her shoulder, and frost magic in her outstretched hand. "Don't come closer," she said, her voice weak.

Usually, fae were a beautiful bunch. All of them with different characteristics, depending on their kingdom, but all of them beautiful. And this female fae was no different. She had long, silver hair, bright blue eyes, and slightly pointed ears. Though she was dressed in rags—dirty pants and sweater—she had a regal air about her. If I could bet, I would say she was royalty or close to it.

Harvey twirled his sword in his hands. "You invaded and destroyed this town. Now, you'll pay for it."

The fae shook her head. "It wasn't me."

Erin stepped in front of Harvey and pushed his blade aside. "What the hell are you doing?" he complained.

Erin took another step closer. "Who was it, then?"

"Shadow fae," she said. "They are after me. I didn't mean to bring them into town, but I had no choice. They chased me off the mountain."

"Shadow fae?" I asked, frowning. As far as I knew, Shadow fae ruled the fae world, and most frost fae had been banished to Earth years ago. "Where are they?"

Suddenly, the young fae pushed her hand out and a flash of frost zipped past my head. I summoned my Dawnblade, ready to kill her on the spot, until I heard the thump right behind me.

A shadow fae encased in ice lay in the hallway a few feet behind me.

"There they are," the fae said.

The shadow fae appeared in the corners of the house. Tall, lean, with long black hair, and either white-porcelain or smooth black skin, the shadow fae surrounded us—four to one. They wore black clothes with hanging fabrics and cloaks, and held on to long black-tipped spears.

Erin held on to the frost fae's arm and hoisted her up. The four of us bunched up as the circle tightened around us.

"Dear Lady Farrah, we've found you," a tall male fae said. His armor was slightly different from the others, with pointed spauldrons and more details in silver. Instead of a spear, he held a long sword in his hand. He was the leader of this bunch. "You should know better than to run from us."

Farrah glanced at us. "Sorry I've put you in danger like this. I didn't want anyone harmed because of me." She took a step forward and spoke louder, "I'll go with General Auron, but only if you promise not to harm my friends."

Friends. She had called us friends. She was trying to trade her life for our safety—for the safety of strangers.

If she didn't have a good heart, then I didn't know who had.

"No." Erin grabbed Farrah's arm. "I don't know what your story is, but it's obvious these guys aren't friendly."

Farrah turned a sorrowful smile to Erin. "I appreciate your concern, but they won't stop hunting me."

I extended my hand and my Dawnblade appeared. I turned my stare to the general. "Then we fight them all and help you out."

Farrah sucked in a sharp breath, as if not believing my words.

General Auron let out a long chuckle. "Demon hunters helping a frost fae. That must be a first." His laughter died and his stare became deadly. "Kill the demon hunters and capture Lady Farrah."

The shadow fae lunged at us. Harvey and I used our swords to fend them off, while Erin fought with her magic for the first time, and Farrah used her frost powers.

It was hard to move in such a tight spot, but once I cut through one of the fae, I was able to push them back and gain more room. Their shadow magic was incredibly powerful, but my magic wasn't too far behind as a half-demon. I threw my darkfire at a shadow fae—it hit him square in the chest and spread like wildfire—then I swung my sword wide and sliced a fae's chest open.

Three down.

I turned around and took the scene in. Harvey had killed two, Farrah had frozen two others, and Erin had created a wall of darkfire around one of them. I knew she was avoiding killing them, but we wouldn't get away if we didn't reduce their numbers drastically.

Erin turned to another shadow fae, and I advanced on her darkfire-encased one. I plunged my sword through the darkfire and killed him, then I turned to the one she was battling. He thrust his spear forward. Erin sidestepped him, but the fae was smart. He sent a shadow bolt at her, anticipating her movement. I wound my arm around her waist, tugged her to me, and twisted her out of the way. Still holding her, I swiped my sword and cut the fae's head off.

Erin turned her face away from the gore, burying her nose in my chest.

If I could have held her like that forever, I would have.

But then shadows spread across the floor like fog.

Farrah yelled, "Get away from it!" She jumped over a side table. After pulling his blade out of a fae's chest, Harvey launched onto an armchair. I jumped to the couch and pulled Erin with me, but tendrils of shadows reached up, winding around her legs and tugging her back.

"No!" I screamed as panic filled my chest.

The shadows wound around Erin's legs and arms, making her immobile, and dragged her back until she stood beside General Auron and the other two remaining fae.

General Auron wrapped a hand around Erin's neck. "Now, Lady Farrah, if you really don't want to see your friend dead, come to me."

Farrah glared at the general. "You're a monster!"

He tsked. "I'm just following orders, my lady."

Her hands clenched into fists. "Then tell Prince Lark he's a monster. And that I'll never marry him."

With a loud scream, Farrah threw her hands out. Dozens, hundreds of ice daggers flew out of her hands and in the direction of the fae and Erin.

My heart dropped, thinking Farrah was going to hit Erin too, but I should have known better. The frost fae guided her ice daggers so they hit everywhere, but where Erin stood. The daggers pierced the two shadow fae from head to toe. Their bodies fell backward and hit the floor in a loud thud.

Still holding Erin, General Auron had created a shadow

shield in front of himself. The ice daggers hit it and melted away instantly.

He dropped the shield and smiled at Farrah. "Impressive, Lady Farrah. But not enough."

"Who says I'm done?" Farrah brought her hands up. The melted ice on the floor shot up in ice spikes around the general. Some pierced through his feet and arms, but none of them hit any essentials parts.

The general grunted. "You insolent bitch ..."

Debilitated, the shadows on the ground retreated, and the tendrils around Erin's arms and legs loosened. I ran to her as the general let her go, and I caught her in my arms before she hit the floor.

"Rey," she whispered, her eyes fixed on mine.

"I've got you," I told her, my heart breaking with all the agony I had just lived through. If Farrah hadn't done something, I would have. "You're safe now."

"Now, General Auron," Farrah said. She brought up more ice around him, making sure he wouldn't be able to escape anytime soon. "You go back and tell Prince Lark that this—" She gestured to all the bodies around us. "—will happen each time he sends his men after me." She lifted her hands above her head and the ice became a prison, enveloping all of him.

Then Farrah fell back on the couch, breathing hard.

I helped Erin up, but the moment she gained her footing, she disentangled herself from me and approached the frost fae. "Your wound," she said, leaning over Farrah's arm. "We need to treat it."

"Right now, what we need is to get out of here," I said. "It'll only be a matter of time before the demon hunters come this way again."

"You're right." Erin nodded. "We can treat her wound on the way."

Harvey frowned. "What? We're helping her now?"

"Didn't she just help us?" Erin asked. "You saw it. The shadow fae were the ones after her. They attacked the town. And they almost killed us too. If it weren't for Farrah, General Auron would have killed me."

Just the thought twisted my gut. "I'm with Erin."

"But she's a supernatural—"

"I know what you're thinking," I said, interrupting Harvey. "That all supernaturals are evil, but that's not true."

"I know that too," Erin said.

Harvey's frown deepened as he glanced at the frost fae. "You did help us just now ..."

"All I want is to get away," Farrah said. "I want to live alone and in peace. But they won't let me."

From what I could gather, Farrah was promised to this Prince Lark, a shadow fae prince, and she didn't want to marry him. If he was as evil and nasty as his general, I could understand why.

"Time to go," I told them.

Erin helped Farrah, who was weak because of her wound and using a lot of her magic. Careful, we exited the house and started down the south road. We aimed for the shadows of the intact buildings, but that wasn't enough.

"What's happening here?"

We all stilled.

Slowly, I turned around and faced Norah. She looked impassive in her dark uniform and the Dawnblade in her hand.

"Norah, I know this looks bad but—"

"But you're helping the innocent fae escape," she said,

cutting me off. Browns pinched, Norah glanced over her shoulder, in the direction of the green. Then she returned her gaze to the wounded fae. "Go quick, before the others come. I'll try to stall them if they come this way."

I stared at her, confuse. "Why are you helping us?" It wasn't normal for a demon hunter to be considerate of supernaturals.

"I have my reasons," Norah said. "Now go, before it's too late." With her hands, she ushered us away.

I wouldn't argue with her. "Let's go," I muttered, grabbing Farrah's arm and helping Erin carry her.

We hobbled to the edge of the town, where Erin, Harvey, and Farrah kept hidden while I went down the side street and picked up my car.

Thankfully, it all went smoothly—I brought my car over, we all got in, and drove away from town. I turned up the air since Erin didn't have a jacket, but she complained that it would be better to keep it chilly for Farrah.

I handed the first aid kit I had gotten from the trunk to Erin, and she worked on cleaning and dressing Farrah's wound. Since it was magical, Farrah probably needed a powerful healing potion, but this was all we could do right now.

Meanwhile, Harvey complained about having to leave his car behind. I almost reached across the seat and punched him. Really? I was more worried about the fact that he was wearing a sweater and Erin had left her jacket when they ran from the restaurant, but he hadn't fucking bothered to offer his sweater to her.

Per Farrah's instructions, I drove around the mountain for a couple of hours, and dropped her off at a hiking trail outside a small town. She promised she would stop to take care of her wounds and eat something before proceeding with her escape.

"Thank you so much," she said, with a soft smile. "It's really good to know there are great demon hunters out there. My wish is that all of them learn from you."

She waved at us, then disappeared into the forest.

"I hope the prince doesn't find her," Erin said, her voice low.

"Me too," I said.

In silence, I drove us back to the academy. It was already past midnight when I parked the car in the underground garage. Harvey and Erin hopped out and started walking away.

I tried holding it in and letting them go, but her name rolled out of my tongue before I could bite it down and hold it in. "Erin ..."

She glanced at me over her shoulder. "What?"

"Can we talk?" I didn't even know what I was going to say to her.

Her brows slammed down. "No."

She wound her arm through Harvey's and resumed walking away with him.

And I stood there, staring at them, as the pit of jealousy inside me only grew bigger, threatening to consume me alive.

9

ERIN

I KNEW IT WAS A DREAM, BUT I COULDN'T WAKE UP, NO MATTER how hard I tried, or wanted.

In my dream, I was alone in a classroom at the academy. I was seated in the middle of the classroom, waiting for the other students and the professor to arrive and for class to start.

Suddenly, the room's light dimmed, bathing the corners in darkness. Two figures stepped out of the darkness. Though I had never seen them before, I knew who they were—Brianne and Cindy. But here, their skin was pale, almost gray, their eyes were dull, and their hair looked like black hay.

They dragged their feet closer to me, limping like zombies.

"Erin, help us," they called out, their voices desperate. "Please, help us."

I didn't get what they wanted help with, until other figures stepped out of the shadows. The demons—a mix of all the ones I had seen so far: garrimps, garrachs, screinors, and muttmaugs—stalked after them.

"Please, Erin, save us."

I stood up and conjured my magic, my darkfire appeared in my open palms. But when I tried to throw it at the demons, they faded away into the air. I tried again and again, but I couldn't control the darkfire.

So, I ran to them.

But I didn't advance. No matter how much I moved my feet and ran, I never got out of the same place.

"Please, Erin!" they cried.

Desperation clashed over me. I opened my mouth to tell them to hang on, but my voice didn't come out.

The demons got them.

I screamed, but no sound came out.

The demons ran their hands across their necks.

Red blood oozed out.

I sat up in my bed, drenched in sweat and breathing hard.

Holy shit, another dream? How many was it now? Six? Seven? Ten? I had lost count.

Since that fight against Asmodeus and finding out the truth about me, and that Brianne and Cindy were my half-sisters, I had been having these crazy nightmares. Each time I was in a normal place—the training grounds, the cafeteria, the classroom—and then Brianne and Cindy arrived, asking for help. Soon, demons appeared and killed them while I could barely move.

These nightmares felt so freaking real.

Exhausted, I reached for my phone on the nightstand and checked the hour. It was three in the morning. I had barely slept three hours. And in another two, I would have to be up to train with my mother.

Holy shit.

I texted my mother: *Can we not train this morning? I'm having a bad night.*

I didn't expect her to reply to me right away, but she did: *I'll give you half an hour more. Meet me at 6.*

Shit.

That wasn't what I wanted. Exhausted and upset, I hugged my pillow and tried to go back to sleep, but all I did was rest my body, because my mind didn't stop.

Of course, the thing I most thought about was Rey. He had been such a jerk last night, with a few tender moments, like when he saved me from the shadow fae's magic, and then broken my fall when General Auron let go of me. But other than that, what the hell? Why had he gone to West Hill? Because of Farrah? I doubted it. He learned about what was happening when he got there.

Then why was he there? It couldn't be because of me, could it? If it was because of me, then I really didn't understand him.

Honestly, I really didn't want to understand him. Right now, all I wanted was to stay away from him. Only then I would be able to forget him and move on.

Reluctantly, I got up at five-thirty and met my mother for training. Because I was so tired and sore, she kicked my butt so hard.

"What is the problem?" she asked, furious with my performance.

I told her I had a nightmare and didn't sleep well. I felt bad not telling her about what had happened last night—she would hear about it eventually, I was sure—and about my nightmares in detail, but at the same time, I didn't want to talk about it with her.

But there was one thing I wanted to talk about. "Why did

you give permission for Harvey to take me out?" I asked her when we were gathering our stuff after training was done.

"Because I think he's a good guy," my mother said, her voice as flat as always. "He comes from a good family, he has a powerful name, and he has a bright future." She paused and a knot showed up between her brows. "Moreover, he knows about your secret and still likes you. It's better like this, to not have to hide the truth from your partner."

I shook my head. "Why are we talking about partners? Can't a woman be alone and happy? I think I'll start a movement. Alone and happy. That's my new motto."

My mother chuckled.

I stared at her as if she was a stranger.

Her smile dissolved. "You're dismissed," she said quickly, pretending nothing happened.

I was still thinking about my mother and chuckles—two things that shouldn't go together—when I joined Claire for our monster identification class an hour later, so I was a little unguarded when Professor Eleanor marched into class and knocked three times on her desk to quiet down the students.

"I'm sure by now many of you heard about the hunt at West Hill last night," she said, her voice serious. "Since we talk about all kinds of supernaturals in this class, I'll tell you exactly what happened last night."

I stiffened. I hadn't even told Claire about it yet. Two desks from me, Harvey leaned back in his chair, as if his mother was talking nonsense.

Ava raised her hand. "I heard several kinds of fae attacked West Hill." She smiled wide, like a psycho. Only a blind person wouldn't see she was trying to do anything she could to gain Professor Eleanor's favor.

"Not several kinds," the professor said. "Only a female

frost fae. She invaded the town and attacked innocent humans. When our demon hunters arrived, she had already destroyed a good part of downtown."

Several gasps bounced through the class.

Claire turned to me and said in a low voice, "You were there last night. What happened?"

"I'll tell you later," I whispered to her.

The professor went on, "After destroying half of West Hill, the fae was able to trick our demon hunters and run. She's now at large and considered very dangerous."

"Leave it to me, professor," Peter exclaimed, sounding enthusiastic. "I'll go after her and kill her."

Harvey slapped his friend's chest, but didn't say anything. Peter snapped at him, and the professor seemed to be fighting an eye roll.

"Although it's unfortunate, this example illustrates what we've been telling you for years," the professor said. "All supernaturals are evil. We might be called demon hunters and hunt mainly demons, but when we can, we protect innocent lives from the rest of the supernaturals."

I frowned, not liking this one bit.

So far, I had met Wyatt, a werewolf, and now Farrah, a frost fae, and they had been nice to me. In fact, I believed Farrah was a great person. Of course, I could be completely mistaken, but I really thought she was trying to live in peace, while the fae prince sent his shadow fae soldiers after her, thus destroying the town and attacking innocent humans. It wasn't her doing.

This mentality had to change, and the first step to that might be in the headmaster's Black Knight Unit. He wanted to bring half-demons to the academy. Once they were accepted, it would only be a matter of time before the entire supernatural world was understood better.

One could only hope ...

Claire and I went to two more classes before sitting at our regular table in the cafeteria. While we ate, I told her all about my date with Harvey, the fire that broke out at the restaurant, which now I believed had been done by the shadow fae, and the demon hunters marching into town and hunting Farrah. I also told her about Farrah, how I had been awestruck by the beautiful frost fae, and how amazing she seemed. And, to finish it up, I told her about Rey ... how he had shown up in town, then saved me and held me, and that it all seemed like pure jealousy.

"So, when he asked to talk to me when we arrived back at the academy, I told him no," I said.

Claire swooned. "I know he's a jerk, but it sure seems like he was jealous."

I groaned. "As if."

"Tell me another reason he would have gone there, then?"

I shrugged. "Maybe I'm mistaken, and he did hear about the fae and went there to help?" But I was sure that wasn't the case. Right now, I was fooling myself, so my heartbreak would be less hurtful.

Suddenly, a shadow fell over me.

I glanced up and saw Ava standing right beside me, her hands on her hips. "I heard all about your date with Harvey last night," she spat, clearly not happy.

What had she heard? That we talked all night? That we had a good time, but as friends? Or had she heard about how we fought shadow fae side by side ... I really doubted that.

"Oh yeah?" I asked, wishing she would leave me alone.

She dropped her arms and balled her hands into fists. "You kissed him, you bitch."

I stood up at that, appalled by her statement. "I did what?"

She snorted. "Now you're trying to deny it? You're really a bitch."

Oh, she was getting on my nerves. "You're the bitch, Ava. Everyone in the academy knows it."

I didn't have time to react. She punched me in the cheek. My head snapped to the side and pain spread over my face. My vision darkened.

Holy shit.

That was it.

When I turned around, I came unloaded. I landed a nice punch to her chin.

"Stop it!" Claire yelled. The rest of the students in the cafeteria took notice and surrounded us, but my focus was on Ava.

She advanced on me, coming with her fists, but I spun around and struck her with a beautiful sidekick to her waist. Groaning, she stumbled back, but only to come at me with a series of fast roundhouse kicks. I deflected most with my forearms, but holy shit, that hurt. She backed me up against a table, and ended up kicking me in the shoulder, before I was able to duck under her leg, and get out of the corner.

Meanwhile, Claire and Harper screamed for us to stop, Stella and Ruby laughed, and the rest of the students cheered us on, joking about bets.

I faked left and she fell for it. Then, I did a series of fast snap kicks, a roundhouse kick, and a back kick, hitting her in the chest and pushing her back. On my fourth kick, she grabbed my leg.

"Hey!" I yelled. That was so damn low.

I was going to jump up and kick her with my other leg, making her lose her grip on me, and land probably on my side on the hard cafeteria floor, but before I could do that, arms closed around my waist and pulled me back.

I thrashed against the firm hold.

"Stop it!" Rey said in my ear.

Instantly, I stopped fighting. A few feet from me, Harvey held Ava. With his arm tight against my waist, Rey dragged me outside the cafeteria, into the cold weather.

Without my jacket, I shivered against him. His hold only tightened.

In silence, Rey took me toward the courtyard with the Blackthorn tree. He wiped a wooden bench clean of ice and snow, and pushed me down on it. Then, he knelt before me and stared at me. His gray eyes, almost silver in this gloomy day, rummaged over me, taking every inch of me, searching for bruises.

His eyes fixed on my cheek. He reached up and ran a thumb over the bruise there. I flinched, not because he had touched me, but because the tenderness quickly became pain again.

"This is going to look nasty later today." He lifted his eyes to mine. "What the fuck were you thinking?" Though his question wasn't nicely phrased, his voice was gentle.

I shrugged. "I wasn't. At the time, I was only feeling furious with her. She was the one who punched me first."

"Let me guess, because of Harvey."

"Why else?" I snorted. "Everything she does is for Harvey and to impress his parents."

Rey sat beside me, a good foot between us. "What about you? Are you trying to impress Harvey too?"

I frowned. Was he really asking me that? I wanted to lie to

him and tell him I was in love with Harvey, and that he confessed to me, and we would get married someday, have several beautiful babies, and live happily ever after.

But I couldn't lie, not to this extent, not to him. So I said the next best thing. "It's none of your business."

Slowly, he nodded. "You're right. It's not."

What was his deal? I wanted to punch him right now. Playing hot and cold like this was killing me. I wished he hadn't pulled me away from Ava, or taken me outside where we were alone, or took care of me. I would rather Ava and I had beaten each other to a pulp, or that someone else had held me back.

The clicking of heels approaching fast got my attention. I glanced past Rey and saw as my mother stomped toward us, her face twisted in a nasty scowl.

"Shit," I whispered, getting up.

Rey stood next to me, but my mother didn't pay him any attention. She pointed her finger at me and said, "You. My office. Now."

With a sigh, I walked past Rey and followed her to the Aster building, where the administrative part of the school was located, including the professors' offices.

She opened the door to her office, let me pass, then slammed it closed.

I was expecting her to walk to her desk, tell me to sit, and talk to me calmly, evenly, and firmly as she always did, but this time, she lost it.

My mother stood right in front of me, a huge knot between her brows. "You and Ava already beat each other up in class several times to the point of being sent to the infirmary. Now you're getting into fights outside of class too? That's unacceptable!"

"She started it!"

"I don't care who started it!" My mother's hands curled into fists. "If she came at you, you should have done your best to dodge her attacks and then leave. Be the bigger person."

"She punched me squared in my face!" I pointed to my cheek, knowing it was already bruised. Rey was right; later it would look much worse. "And you want me to just walk away? My blood isn't that cold."

"Then you have to learn to make your blood cold," my mother said. "You have to try harder."

"What the hell is this about?" I put my hands on my waist. "I don't care if the others think I'm crazy and unstable. Why do you care about my image in school? Are you worried about your image? You shouldn't. It's not like anyone knows you're my mother."

My mother's face turned red with rage. "Watch your mouth, Erin!"

"Ha." I scoffed. "I'm nineteen, not nine. Your chance to tell me things like that is long past."

I started for the door.

My mother grabbed my wrist. "We're not done here."

I jerked free of her grip. "Don't worry. If you think I'm an embarrassment to you, all you need to do is keep quiet. That way, no one will find out I'm your daughter." I narrowed my eyes, thinking. "If you want, you can completely disassociate from me. You can pass me to another advisor, and we stop meeting for training. There. Then your contact with me will only be during class and no one will ever suspect anything."

I walked out of her office.

"Erin!" she called, but I closed the door and kept on moving, one foot in front of the other, until I had descended the stairs and was back outside in the cold.

I stared at the Blackthorn tree in the middle of the courtyard.

I didn't know what my mother wanted from me. She had given me nothing my entire life, and now she wanted me to be a model daughter?

In her dreams.

Feeling like a failure, I shoved my hands inside the pockets of my jacket and walked to the Gardenia building, where I buried myself in my room for the rest of the day.

10

REY

DESPITE GOING TO CLASS LIKE A NORMAL STUDENT EVERY DAY, I mostly felt like I was more than just a student at the academy. Because of my duties with campus security and my deal with Randall, there were perks and obligations well above any student.

But there were days when school drama surrounded me, and I felt like a normal student.

I had signed up for weapon forging again this semester, and to my surprise, Erin had too. Claire was in here too, and had been her partner since the first day of classes.

And I was left with Tanner, the douche who was paying too much attention to Claire.

I didn't have time to care about others' opinions and what they did, but I had gotten to know Claire, and thought she was a good person. She was cute, had a good heart, and was a great friend to Erin.

Because of that, I worried about how lovestruck she seemed whenever Tanner looked her way.

"Today, we'll be working with several kinds of metal,"

Professor Astrid said. "We'll grab a piece of each and apply heat to them, try to mold them, get a feel for them. You'll soon see what metal is best for each kind of weapon."

I grunted on the inside. This was basic, and I had learned a thing or two about metals centuries ago. But since Professor Astrid didn't know how old I was and I needed a good grade, I went to the storage room in the back of the classroom, and picked out pieces of several kinds of metal.

Tanner leaned over me while I examined the steel section. "Hey, partner, got all the metal we need?"

I glared at him. "You can get yours yourself."

He wound his arm over my shoulders. "But we're doing this together."

I ducked under his arm. "Touch me again, and you'll lose a fucking finger."

Already irritated, I walked out of the storage room, only to almost bump into Erin.

"Sorry," she muttered. She didn't look at me once while she took a large step to the side and walked past me.

I frowned. Why the fuck did that hurt so much? I should be glad she was acting like I was a stranger.

Even so, I couldn't deny hating to see how purple the mark on her cheek was now. Ava had really gotten her. But I had seen Ava earlier this morning, and I was glad to say, Erin left a good bruise on her face too.

I returned to my assigned forge, and placed all the metal pieces I had picked out on the table. A minute later, Tanner showed up carrying pieces for himself—but the dumbass had gotten several of the same.

"Let's get to work," Tanner said with a grin.

I knew what he wanted. For me to start so he could copy me. I knew his reputation. Ever since he joined the academy,

Tanner had been arrogant, acted like he was the best, and exploited his classmates.

This semester, I had been assigned to forge number twelve, the same as last semester. Erin and Claire had been assigned to forge number eleven, right beside mine.

Despite my best efforts to ignore her, my attention was always divided between whatever I was doing and whatever Erin was doing. We were in our third week of classes, and I had butted in on her work twice already. What could I do? I couldn't resist. When I saw her making a mistake that would cost her a lot of work, or even sometimes hurt her, I had to tell her.

Erin and Claire brought the pieces of metal to their tables. Instantly, Tanner leaned over ours, his elbow on the top, and his chin on his hand, and smiled wide at Claire.

Claire's cheeks turned red.

Shaking my head, I started working. On the table beside ours, the girls started working too. But Tanner remained in the same position, flirting with Claire, who tried to help Erin, but couldn't resist stealing glances at Tanner every few seconds.

I had already tested five different metals, when finally Tanner moved and picked up a piece of cheap iron. He walked around the table and stood right beside me.

"She's cute, right?" Tanner asked, his eyes still on Claire.

"Leave her alone, Tanner," I said.

"Why?" He sounded appalled. "She's single. I'm single. I think we would make a good pair."

"Listen, you—"

I shut my mouth when Claire walked back to the storage room and Tanner went after her, ignoring the warning I was about to give him.

Really? He was going to trail after her like that? Claire deserved better.

Even more irritated than before, I dropped the piece of steel I was messing with and took a step to follow them.

Erin's arm shot out in front of me. "Don't you dare."

I glanced at her. "What?"

"I noticed you were watching Tanner and Claire," she said, her tone harsh. "I don't know what your deal is. Maybe you're into Claire too, but back off now. Tanner was here first."

My brows furrowed. "You think I'm into Claire?"

"Why else would you care if Tanner flirted with her? If they start dating?"

"Because Tanner is a douche."

She crossed her arms and jutted her chin out. "Like some other guys I know."

Holy fuck. I ran a hand through my hair. "I know I'm a jerk and I already told you to stay away from me, but I need to tell Claire to stay away from Tanner."

"No, you don't need to do anything." Erin shook her head. "As her best friend, I'll take care of her. She's happy now and excited about him. Leave them alone. If I suddenly think Tanner is a jerk too, I'll do something about it."

She spun around and turned her attention back to the metal on the table.

I hated that she was right, but I backed the fuck off. For the rest of the class, I did my best to ignore when Tanner openly flirted with Claire, and she fell into his trap.

After weapon forging class, I had a free period, so I walked around campus and checked the guards' outpost to ensure everything was running smoothly, then stopped by the library to get started on a project from demon history class.

I picked up a handful of books on the subject and sat at a table in the corner, from where I could see most of the place —my protective instincts were always on.

Not even five minutes later, Harper sat down beside me.

I stared at her, wondering what the fuck she wanted with me? Besides one time when I took her to the infirmary because the professor had asked, I hadn't talked to her at all.

But I knew she had been around Erin and Claire the past few days.

"So, Rey, how are classes going?" Harper asked.

"Hm, fine."

"Good." She nodded. "Oh, I see you're working on the Dark Days War. It's for demon history, right? I remember my sister studying it when she was at the academy. Do you need help?"

I frowned. Harper's sister, Holly, was six years older than her and had graduated from the academy some time ago. She now worked in Chasseur Ville because she didn't want to join the Blackthorn Hunters.

"No, I'm good."

"Hm ..." She glanced around. "So ..."

I let out a long sigh. "Harper, I can see there's something on your mind. Spill it."

Her cheeks reddened. "Shit," she muttered. "All right. Okay. See ... I know you're good friends with Claire—"

"I wouldn't say I'm good friends with her, but okay."

"—and I wanted to ask you if you know if she likes someone."

Wait. Where was this going?

Erin and Claire entered the library and settled at a table

in the middle of the room. Harper's hazel eyes twinkled as she stared at Claire.

That was when it struck me.

Harper liked Claire.

As if a bad romantic comedy was playing, Tanner walked into the library. He sat down at the table beside Claire and Erin, and turned his flirtatious gaze to Claire, who obviously had a hard time focusing because of him.

"Harper," I started, feeling bad for her. "Claire is into Tanner."

Harper's shoulders deflated. "I noticed he was flirting with her, but I think this is the first time I've seen her respond to him like that."

Then she was fucking blind, because Claire had been mooning over him for a couple of weeks now.

"I'm sorry," I said, feeling awkward about it. I hadn't had friends in so long, with the exception being Harvey, that saying things like that and feeling sympathy for others made me feel weird.

She shrugged and plastered a fake smile on her face. "It's okay. It is what it is."

Without another word, Harper got up. She stopped by her table, grabbed her things, and walked out of the library.

When Harvey arrived and sat down with Tanner so he could flirt with Erin, I decided this really was a fucking romantic comedy.

Before my temper spiked, I picked up my things and walked out too.

11

ERIN

FOR A WEEK, MY MOTHER LET ME PLAY THE REBELLIOUS daughter and skip the early morning trainings. But then she invaded my room and dragged me out of my bed.

"You seem to have forgotten that you're unlike any other demon hunter," she said, as she threw my uniform at me. "You're the daughter of the Supreme Demon. You need to train harder than anyone else."

I frowned, trying to think of something clever to say to her, to rebel for a few more minutes, but my brain was still foggy with sleep.

Besides, I agreed with her.

It had been almost three months since Asmodeus told me I was King Brikan's daughter, and no other demon had come for me yet. The quiet was unsettling.

During winter break, I asked my mother about my father several times, but she always answered with the same thing: She had been young and stupid. She believed his lies and let him trick her. That was it. She never told me anything else.

This morning during training, it wasn't any different. I

asked her if she had any idea why he was so quiet. I mean, I knew about it now. Why didn't he just barge into the academy and take me? He certainly had the power to do it.

Once more, she ignored me.

Usually when I left training and went back to the Gardenia building to take a shower and have breakfast before classes, the school was still quiet. But not this morning. It was freaking cold out, and there were already a bunch of girls hanging around the courtyard, which had been cleared of snow overnight.

Not caring about them, I went to my room, took a warm shower, put on my uniform and a thick jacket, then met Claire in the cafeteria for breakfast.

Here too, the place looked busier, with more students walking around and chatting animatedly.

"What's going on?" I asked as I sat beside Claire at our usual table. I placed my tray in front of me and sipped from my coffee.

"The Blackthorn Hunters are arriving on campus this morning," Claire said.

I frowned. "Why? Did something happen?"

"Not yet." She turned a full-on smile at me. "They are coming to prepare for the Spring Hunter's Dance."

"The what?"

Claire chuckled. "I love it that you don't know a lot about our world, and I have to relive the excitement of finding out about them with you."

"I don't love it," I said, trying to pretend I was insulted, but that only made her chuckle.

"The Spring Hunter's Dance is an annual ball here at the school, honoring the best full-fledged hunters. Students are chosen to help the hunters and plan the ball." She gestured to the eager girls around the cafeteria. "As you can see, everyone is hoping to get picked."

I raised my eyebrows at her. "Are you?"

She nodded. "Of course I am. Being chosen would be an immense honor."

If she said so. I didn't see anything great about helping plan a ball.

We finished eating breakfast and walked across campus to our first class of the day. But before we arrived in the Orchid building, the entire campus had gathered in the courtyard.

"What's happening now?" I asked as Claire insisted we joined the others.

A moment later, the headmaster stepped out of the Aster building, followed by a group of men and women dressed in sleek black leather armor.

The Blackthorn Hunters.

As if we were at a concert, the students in the courtyard cheered and applauded, including Claire. It seemed the Blackthorn Hunters were more famous in our society than I realized. From the hysterical way Stella and Ruby screamed, I would say they were more famous than rock stars.

The demon hunters waved and bowed their heads in acknowledgment. I recognized Doreen with the other hunters, but I had no idea who the others were. If they had been in West Hill that night and seen me, I didn't remember them.

After a couple of minutes, the headmaster and the hunters went back inside the Aster building, but the students remained in the courtyard, as if waiting for them to come back.

I rolled my eyes. "Let's go to class."

I had to practically drag Claire to class. Everyone else was late, and the professor was pissed. Like me, she didn't seem to think having the hunters visit was a big deal.

The day was weird. We did all the normal things—classes and lunch—but everyone seemed too wired to slow down. There was more chatter everywhere, and the lectures had been slower because of it.

Claire and I were back in the cafeteria and had finished lunch when one of the academy's secretaries showed up and told me to go to the headmaster's office immediately.

My first thought was that I was in trouble. My second thought was that he was calling me to check on my mission or give me another one. But he wouldn't send for me in the middle of the day when there were other students around, would he?

"Oh, you were one of the chosen," Claire said, sounding excited.

"What?" I asked, lost.

"Look!" She pointed to the secretary, who was a few tables from ours, talking to another student. Then, she moved on and talked to someone else. "She's telling the chosen ones." Claire grabbed my hand. "Holy crap, this is great."

I frowned. "Want to take my place?"

Claire gasped. "I would if I could. Now go." She pushed me off my seat. "She did say immediately."

Reluctantly, I got up from my seat and went to the Aster building. The door to the headmaster's office was open, and he welcomed me with a big smile. "Come in, Erin."

I paused once I stepped inside. There were a few students gathered in front of his desk, including Ava. But what had made me stop were the Blackthorn Hunters who had taken seats at the long black glass table on the other side of the room. They really did seem like an impressive and powerful bunch. Among them, Doreen caught my eye. She winked at me.

Other students entered the office, and I woke up from my daze and joined them all in front of the headmaster's desk.

Not long after, the headmaster closed the door and said, "As you may have guessed, you have been chosen to help the Blackthorn Hunters organize the ball." He walked behind his desk but didn't sit down. "You'll meet as often as you see fit to get it done before the ball date." He picked up a sheet of paper from his desk. "I'll now pair you up with the hunters you'll work with. You're welcome to use the larger meeting room across the hallway to talk. Demon Hunter Andre, you're with Taylor Smith." A hunter with dark skin and long dreadlocks stood up. Taylor, a third-year student, turned to him. They both walked out of the room and went to the meeting room. "Demon Hunter Doreen, you're with Ava Heyward." I heard Ava's grunt as she stepped forward and joined Doreen. What? She had a specific hunter in mind? The headmaster read a couple more names, then finally I heard mine. "Demon Hunter Thierry, you're paired with Erin Delman."

A tall hunter with short black hair and brown eyes stood up. He walked to me, and together, we left the headmaster's office and walked into the meeting room. The other hunters and students were seated around the long table—with over twenty chairs—talking about the ball.

Thierry gestured to one of the table's ends, where no one was seating.

He pulled a chair for me, then took the seat beside mine.

With a half-smile, he offered his hand to me. "Hi, I'm Thierry."

I stared at his hand for a moment before taking it. "I'm Erin."

"Nice to meet you, Erin."

"Ditto." I pulled my hand away, feeling awkward about this.

His smile widened. I stared, honestly taken aback by him. He was young, probably in his mid-twenties, and cute. All right, who was I kidding? He was handsome and strong. Manly. Holy shit, I felt like a horny teenage thinking like that about a stranger, but it was true.

"So, the ball," he started. Even his voice was rough and charged.

"Hm, let me just tell you, I'm new to all of this, so I have no idea what we're doing."

Thierry frowned. "What do you mean?"

I sighed and told him a simple version of my story: that I had been raised away from this society, but after demons attacked me and killed my aunt, I was brought to the academy. I had lived here for six months and still didn't know the ins and outs.

"That's refreshing," he said.

"Not as much as this ball." I grabbed a notebook and pen from my tote bag. "So, what should we be organizing?"

"The ball can wait," he said, staring straight at me. "I want to know more about you."

I frowned, not sure how to feel about his attention. "Hm, there's nothing special about me." What a lie. But what made me special, also made me a target, so I stayed quiet.

"I doubt that." Thierry reached over the table and took my hand in his. "You're lively and beautiful. Tell me you're a good student and a great fighter, and I'm yours."

I stared at him, at his hand in mine, not sure what to say.

He was a strong hunter. If he had made the main group, it meant he had been an excellent student. He couldn't be a bad guy if he battled to save our world, right? Besides, he was handsome too.

Things hadn't worked out with Rey, and there was no spark with Harvey. Maybe Thierry was the one? I shook my head. What the hell was I thinking? Hadn't I resigned myself to be single and happy?

However, something about him coming on so strong five seconds after meeting me rubbed me the wrong way.

"I'm an okay student."

He narrowed his eyes at me. "I doubt that." He pulled my hand to him, making me lean over the table.

Then, he kissed the top of my hand.

I froze.

"Erin."

I heard the growl in his voice when he called my name.

I pulled my hand away and turned as Rey stomped toward us. "Rey, what are you doing here?"

"Hey, Rey," Thierry said. "Haven't seen you in a while. How is it going?"

Rey turned his fuming silver eyes to Thierry. "What the fuck do you think you're doing?"

Thierry lost the amused smile. "What do you mean?"

"You're supposed to be planning the ball, not flirting with a student," Rey said, as if he was the boss.

"Have you looked at her?" Thierry gestured to me. "It's hard to focus on anything other than her when she's so close."

My cheeks warmed, but I felt a little icky about the whole thing. "Hm, I—"

"I don't care what you think," Rey snapped. "If you don't

stop flirting and get to work, I will report you to Randall. I'm sure he wouldn't mind switching her for a *male* student."

"What the hell? We'll get the job done even if I'm flirting with her."

"I would rather you didn't flirt with her.

Thierry stood up, his chest puffed. "This does not concern you."

"What if it does?" Rey leaned closer.

I stood between them both before they started a fight. "This is ridiculous. Can you two stop it?"

"I will stop it once Thierry backs down."

Thierry balled his hands. "Make me."

"That's enough," the headmaster's voice boomed through the room. We all turned to him. To my surprise, the room was empty and the headmaster stood by the door, his eyes hard. "Rey, go to my office." Rey hesitated, but then he put his tail between his legs and walked out. The headmaster looked at Thierry. "As a Blackthorn hunter, I expect a professional attitude from you."

"Yes, sir," Thierry said with a nod of his head.

The headmaster glanced at me for a second before walking out the room.

I sat down in my chair, my mind reeling. What the hell had just happened? Thierry had openly flirted with me, Rey lost it, and even the headmaster interfered.

It had all been a crazy dream, right?

Thierry sat beside me again. "I'm sorry. I didn't mean to be disrespectful or cause a scene, but I won't take it back. You've enchanted me and I'll make sure you know it." He grabbed my notebook and pen. "But first, let's get to work."

* * *

BECAUSE I HAD BEEN CHOSEN TO BE ONE OF THE BALL organizers, I ended up missing one of my classes in the afternoon, so I had to go to the library to copy Claire's notes and study, before dinnertime.

When I briefly met her between classes, she had grilled me about the meeting. Who I had been paired with? What were we in charge of? When would we meet again? I hadn't told her about Rey and Thierry's showdown because there was no time. And because I really didn't want to think about it right now. I would tell her later tonight or tomorrow ...

The gray day was turning black when I finally made it out of the Iris building and headed to the cafeteria.

However, Rey exited the Statice building and halted in my path.

"We need to talk," he said, his voice grave.

I didn't stop. "If it's about Thierry, I don't want to hear it."

"Erin, listen to me." Rey walked with me. "Thierry is a good guy, yes, but he's not the dating type. You two wouldn't work out."

That boiled my blood. I skidded to a stop and faced him. "Let's get one thing clear: I don't care what you think. If I want to date Harvey or Thierry or even Tanner, that is none of your business. You're the one who rejected me, who told me you didn't like me, so leave me alone."

"But—"

"No." I raised my finger at him, as if I was fending him off. "You have to stop. If you don't like me, then leave me alone. You're confusing me when you suddenly show up when I'm having a date with a guy, or start an argument with another one who is flirting with me. You can't do that. Please, just ... pretend I don't exist. That's what I'm trying to do with you."

Though it hurt to say the words, though it hurt to see the flatness in his eyes, as if my words hadn't affected him at all, I knew it had to be done. I had to get it—him—out of my system.

If he wanted me to let go of him, he needed to let me go too.

Without looking back, I walked away.

12

REY

THAT NIGHT, I COULDN'T SLEEP. I WAS SO PISSED WITH MYSELF, with everything, that it took me a long time to calm down my fucking brain and finally rest.

After calling me out of the meeting room, Randall hadn't done much. He said he was upset with my attitude, but Thierry had been inappropriate. He gave me a warning and promised to talk to Thierry later.

The next morning, I went to monster identification. This was one of the mixed grade elective classes, and Erin was in it too.

"Today's class is a little different," the professor said. "I've hidden gems of different colors on campus. Your job is to locate them. But not any gem. The color specific to you and your partner." She showed us a leather pouch. "Pick a coin. The color on the coin will indicate your team. Pair up and go find the gem."

I frowned, not sure of the purpose of this scavenger hunt.

Erin grabbed the coin before me. Hers was gold. Then

Taylor got a red coin, Harper got a blue one, and Peter grabbed a pink one.

And of course, I fished a gold coin from the pouch. "You've got to be kidding me," I muttered, glaring at the coin.

Erin stared at the coin in my hand with wide eyes. She approached the professor and asked, "Can I swap my coin with someone else?"

"No time for that," the professor said, messing with her wristwatch. "Now go! The first team to come back with their gem wins!"

"What do we get?" Peter asked, always worried about the grand prize.

"Glad you asked," the professor said. "The winning team will get extra credit and five points on the next test."

Everyone filed from the classroom in a rush to search for their gems, but Erin and I stayed back, frozen in place.

"We should split up to look for it," Erin said.

I didn't need extra credit or points, but for some reason, I thought this game was just what we needed to mend things between us. Not that I should be trying to mend anything. I deserved her hate, but I honestly didn't like it. I would rather we broke things off completely between us, but without so much argument or heartbreak.

If, at the end of the day, we could be good acquaintances, I would be glad.

I shook my head. "And how will you warn me if you find it? Or vice versa?"

She dropped the coin on her desk and started picking up her stuff. "Then you can do it alone."

"Erin ..."

She lifted her eyes at me. "Don't Erin me. We already talked about this last night."

"I know, I know, but I don't really like things half-done. Let's just search for the fucking gem. The sooner we go, the sooner we'll be done with it."

I hoped she noticed the forlorn tone of my voice and how I wasn't interested in this either, and ended up agreeing to be done with the task.

Apparently it worked because she sighed and said, "All right. Let's get this over with."

Together, we walked out of the building. The sun peeked from behind the clouds, trying to warm up the chilly day a little. It wasn't working. At least, the campus had been magically cleared of snow—because of the Blackthorn Hunters' visit yesterday. Though it was mid-February now. There was still a chance we would see a lot more snow before the season was over.

"Where could this gem be hidden?" I asked, looking at the courtyard in front of us.

Erin shrugged. "I don't know." The harshness of her tone, as if she would rather die than be around me, cut through my chest.

Sometimes I hated my fucking resolution to keep my distance from her. Or rather, trying to. I was doing a fucked up job.

The gem wouldn't be hidden so close to us, so easy. The best bet was to search the building and look for it on the lawn, in bushes, and in trees before the outer walls.

"This way," I said, taking the lead. I started around the Statice building, and Erin followed me, purposely lagging.

We walked slowly, looking around the ground, the cracks in the stone pavement, the windowsills, the empty flowerbeds lining the buildings, and in bushes. We did find the pink gem underneath a tree's root, but there was no sign of the gold gem anywhere.

After about thirty minutes walking behind the Gardenia and Snapdragon buildings, Erin and I made our way back to the center of campus.

I looked around the courtyard. "It can't be here."

"Why not?" Erin walked ahead, eager to end this partnership.

"It would be too obvious."

"One more reason to hide it here, then." She took slow steps toward the center, searching under wooden benches and patches of thick grass, until she stopped right in front of the Blackthorn tree. "I gotta admit, this tree is impressive."

I stood beside her and looked up at the tree. A thick, black trunk, and hundreds of thin branches and vines, all covered in thorns. The thing was massive, bold, and powerful.

"Indeed it is," I muttered. My eyes scanned its trunk, thinking the professor could have hidden the gem behind the vines, but I found something else instead. "What is this?" I reached over and ran my fingers over what seemed to be a loose piece of shiny wood interwoven in the vines and thorns. I gasped. "This is a blade."

Erin frowned. "What do you mean?"

I tried removing the piece of wood, but it didn't budge. "This is odd." I grabbed the tip of the blade and pulled, but again, it didn't move.

"What are you trying to do?" Erin reached for it. Her fingers brushed against mine as she grabbed the tip of the weapon. I quickly pulled my hand back.

Then she pulled the blade out. She held it with both her hands and stared at it, her eyes wide. "This ..."

I nodded. "It's a raw piece of an original Dawnblade. Just like Randall's." It was a special blade, a mix of metal and dark wood. Holy fuck, I hadn't seen one like that in centuries. In fact, besides Randall's, I had only heard about the others, not seen any. "It chose you."

Erin's brows curled down. "What?"

"The Dawnblade. I couldn't get it, but it easily came off for you. It's your Dawnblade."

She stared at the piece in her hands, as if doubting it. "Why?"

I shrugged. "I don't know, but this is special." I grabbed one of her hands in mine and tugged her with me. "Let's go. We need to forge your Dawnblade right now."

There were two classrooms with forges in the Orchid building. One was occupied with a current class. The other was empty. I pushed Erin in, closed the door, and locked it.

"Why all this secrecy?" she asked, still holding the crude blade.

"We all have to forge our Dawnblades the normal way now," I explained as I made my way to the forges on the back of the room. "Randall is probably the only demon hunter alive with a Dawnblade like that. It's a rare thing and it might mean something."

"Like this mark." Erin turned her hand over and tugged the sleeve of her jacket up, showing off the sign on her wrist that marked her as a daughter of the king of the underworld. "And ..." She glanced down to her chest. "Never mind."

She was going to mention the soul bond. I was sure of it. But I was thankful she didn't. If she told me about hers, I wasn't sure I would be able to stay quiet about mine.

"Come on, let's make you a Dawnblade."

At that, her lips tugged up a tiny bit, but enough to make

my heart skip a fucking beat. She was so fucking beautiful and amazing ... it took all my strength not to embrace her right then.

To tell her how I really felt.

To kiss her.

I reined my desire and feelings in and turned to the forge.

Because it was her sword, I guided her through each of the steps, but I let her do it all herself. When necessary, I gave her a hand. Otherwise, I stayed away. This was such a special blade, I wanted her to feel proud of it—not only because the tree had given the sword to her, but because she had been the one to make it.

The Dawnblade wasn't made the same way a normal sword was, and this Dawnblade was even more elaborate. We had to reshape the odd mix of wood and metal that formed the blade, create a hilt—which Erin insisted looked like the vines and thorns from the Blackthorn tree, add the indentation around the pommel that would later be occupied by magical gems, and then infuse it with magic.

One of the forges had a magical core—Randall never told us how that worked, and no one dared to mess with it—so hours later, when we were sweaty and tired, Erin put her almost-done-blade inside that forge. Instantly, the magic enveloped the sword, glowing a bright white light and illuminating the entire room.

When the shine was gone, I said, "It's done."

With a satisfied glow in her eyes, Erin picked up the sword from the forge. "It's beautiful," she whispered.

It really was. The blade was long and slightly curved, resembling a scythe. The material was unique—a mix of magical wood from the tree and metal. The hilt looked like several vines interwoven, and thorns lined the pommel, leaving enough space between them for the gems that would come later. When Erin twirled it in her hand, a dark glow covered the blade.

I had an idea. "Wait, it's not ready yet." I reached for her Dawnblade, but stopped before I touched it. "May I?" She nodded and handed me the sword. I lay the sword on its side in my open palms. "Now, rest your hands over mine." Erin frowned, but she did it. Our hands touched, with the blade sandwiched between our skins. "Now, infuse it with your magic. That way, your Dawnblade will be even more special and unique."

She closed her eyes and sent her magic into her sword. I stared at her, and sent my magic too. If she was my soulmate as the twin soul bond said, then my magic would be compatible with hers, and welcomed inside her blade.

We pushed our magics into the blade. It hummed with so much magic, but it held firm and true, even better than I expected.

Soon, I reared my magic back and pushed the sword toward Erin. "It's ready now. Congratulations on your amazing Dawnblade."

She looked up at me, her smile wide and true. "Thank you." She held her blade by the hilt.

"Now, do it," I urged her. "Make it disappear and appear like we do."

She frowned. "How?"

I stretched my arm beside me. "I just think about it." My Dawnblade appeared in my hand. "Then I imagine it gone." My sword faded into thin air.

Erin cleared her throat and spread her legs apart, as if she was getting ready for a fight.

I thought she wouldn't get it at first, but I should have

known better. The moment she extended her arm beside her, the sword was gone. A moment later, it appeared again.

"I did it," she cried, her pitch high. Happy.

I nodded. "You have a special connection with your sword. Treasure it well."

"I will." She glanced at the blade a moment before it disappeared again. She turned her bright smile to me, making my fucking heart wrench again. "Thank you."

"My pleasure," I told her. "But just remember. This is a special Dawnblade. For now, don't let others know you have one like that."

Her grin diminished. "I understand."

As much as I wanted to spend the rest of the evening and night hidden away with her, my resolution of being civil and not doing anything stupid only went so far. I needed to get away from her now.

"We should go before we're considered missing," I said.

Erin nodded. "Right."

Together, we walked out of the classroom. The sun was almost set, and the entire school was quieting down for dinner and curfew.

Feeling like my will was fading, I didn't escort her to the Gardenia building. Instead, I bid her a quick goodnight outside the Orchid building and went for a walk around the Lotus lake at the academy's northeast corner.

The fresh air would be good for my mind.

But there was nothing that could cure my fucking aching heart.

13

It had been stupid of me, but after the day Rey and I spent several hours forging my Dawnblade, I thought we had turned a new leaf. We had bonded that day, even if not romantically, but as friends, as buddies. Despite all the shit going on between us, that day showed me we could still get along fine. I had even told Claire everything about it—the sword, the forging, the bonding—and she had agreed with me.

Until that day was gone and he avoided me again. A week and a half passed and I only saw him in class, and even then he barely looked my way or talked to me.

Really?

Sometimes I wondered if he was almost a thousand years old. He was acting more like a sixteen-year-old boy.

Claire and I had just left the cafeteria after lunch when the air around the academy started bustling. Girls ran amok and shrieked as if they were about to see their idols.

Oh, that meant the Blackthorn Hunters were back at the

academy. Sure enough, I soon received a note to meet with Thierry in the Aster building.

This time, he was waiting for me in the lobby.

"Erin, I missed you," he said, sounding so sincere, it spooked me.

"Shall we work?" I asked, showing him the notebook I brought.

Per the headmaster's request, we went to an empty, smaller meeting room on the first floor and started working on our task: the guests' list.

I started writing down the names of all the full-fledged Blackthorn Hunters. Thirty-four of them were stationed in the mountains, but I then learned that there were many other outposts around the world.

Thierry told me that though Randall had settled in the United States and opened an academy here, he had lived all over the world, and had established several smaller units of the Blackthorn Hunters. For this ball, many of these hunters would come.

"Not all of them, though," Thierry said. "After all, we need hunters to stay put in case they are needed."

I guess that made sense. Next, I started writing down the hunter's immediate family members.

That sparked a question. "What about you, Thierry? Where's your family?"

So far, he had been smiling and flirting with me as much as the first time I had met him. But with that question, Thierry straightened and grew serious.

"I come from a prestigious demon hunter family, though my parents were killed during a battle a few years ago."

"I'm sorry," I whispered, feeling for him. Knowing how terrible it was to lose someone special, I understood his pain.

"Before that, I was always considered the golden boy of the academy," he said, and to my surprise, there wasn't a hint of arrogance in his voice. He was just being sincere. "People loved me. Well, I guess they still do."

I snorted. "You should have seen the girls earlier. Whenever you hunters step foot in the academy, they swoon so hard."

He tilted his head, his hazel eyes fixed on mine. "What about you? Did you swoon?"

How to answer that? Should I play this game? Should I flirt with him? My mind went directly to Rey, but my heart wilted. Why was I thinking about the jerk who had rejected me?

I could try this. I could flirt back. What was the worst that could happen? If in the long run I decided it wouldn't work, then I would back off.

Just like it with Harvey.

Wasn't that part of life?

But I thought about breaking Thierry's heart, the same way Rey had broken mine time and time again, and I hated it. I hated giving him hope without being sure of my feelings.

In the end, I decided to take a step forward, but still hold back somehow. "Maybe."

His smile widened. "I'll take it."

I glanced at the list in my notebook. I thought for a minute, then started adding the name of the professors, the staff, and their families.

For some reason, my mind ran wild, and I thought of which professors had been full-fledged demon hunters before having to step down. Professor Eleanor, Harvey's mother, was one of them. Like many of them, she also had lost her ability to be a demon hunter during a battle against a demon—Asmodeus, Rey's father.

Which made me think of another question ...

"Have you had any exciting missions so far?" I asked, not sure exciting was the right word when you were risking your life. "I mean, you're pretty young ..."

"I graduated four years ago," he said. That put him in the range of twenty-six years old, exactly how old I thought he was. "So I've been on many exciting missions. The one I'm working on right now is pretty exciting, if not puzzling."

"Can you tell me what it's about, or are the details confidential?"

He chuckled. "Nah, I guess I can tell. I'm leading a chase for a fae. A female frost fae, actually." My heart stopped. "A few weeks ago, she was in West Hill. She destroyed half of the town. I'm sure your professors talked to you about it."

They had, but more than that, I had seen it. I had lived it. Only Doreen had seen Harvey and me there. A few more hunters had seen Rey, but since Rey was well known among them, they didn't think much of it.

"Yeah, I heard about it," I muttered.

"She escaped somehow, but it doesn't matter. I'll find her someday and kill her."

My stomach dropped.

Oh no.

I opened my mouth to tell him it hadn't been Farrah who had destroyed the town. I wanted to tell him it had been the shadow fae. I also wanted to tell him Farrah had saved me from them.

And I had helped her escape.

If I told him that, he would report me to the headmaster.

Worse, I would be interrogated by Thierry and the other hunters. They would think I was an accomplice and punish me.

Shit, I couldn't say anything.

I shut my mouth again, and for the rest of the afternoon, I focused on creating the long guest list, and nothing else.

* * *

WHEN I GOT BACK TO MY ROOM AFTER MY MEETING WITH Thierry, Claire was waiting for me by my door.

"You won't guess what just happened," she said, practically jumping up and down with excitement, making her cute curls bounce.

I unlocked the door. "What?"

We stepped into the room. Claire closed the door and leaned against it. "Tanner asked me out." She squealed.

I smiled at her. "That's great."

In truth, I wasn't so sure how great that was. In the last ten days, I had paid more attention to the guy, and unfortunately, I started becoming a little wary of him. I blamed Rey for instilling the doubt bug in my mind. If he hadn't showed me how upset he was about Tanner, I wouldn't have paid attention.

But I did, and I had seen how arrogant he could be. In front of Claire, he was kind and gentle, always smiling at her. Once she turned around, he scowled at everyone and treated them as if he was better than them. I had even seen him yelling at one of the kitchen staff the other day.

I had been meaning to talk to her about him, but I could

never find a good moment. And now that he had finally asked her out, I felt bad for bringing it up.

My only hope was that Tanner matured soon. That he was a great guy to Claire and stopped being such a self-absorbed brat.

"We're going on a date soon," she said, her green eyes twinkling. "Will you help me get ready?"

"Of course," I said, thinking of when she had helped me get ready for my date with Harvey. "We can ask Harper for her stilettos again."

"Oh no." Claire shook her head. "I could never walk in those heels."

I chuckled. "We can borrow them early and start practicing."

We made other silly comments like that while I put away my books and organized my things for the next day. Then, we both headed downstairs to eat dinner.

"Oh, wait," Claire said, stopping in the middle of the staircase. "I forgot something in my room."

I frowned. "What?"

"Something Tanner gave me." She started backing up. "Go ahead, I'll meet you there in a couple of minutes." She rushed up the stairs.

I shook my head, a little worried. I wanted her to be happy, but I wondered if she would be truly happy with Tanner.

After a long exhale, I went down the rest of the stairs. I was crossing the lobby, heading toward the cafeteria, when I heard soft sniffles. I paused, thinking I was mistaken, but I heard it again.

On instinct, I followed the noise to a corner of the lobby,

where a hallway opened to the back of the building and led to the back door.

There, seated on the floor with her back against the wall, was Harper.

"What happened?" I asked, kneeling beside her.

She wiped at her eyes. "Nothing."

"It doesn't seem like nothing."

Her eyes filled with tears again. "It's silly."

For some reason, I wanted her to talk to me. Maybe it was sympathy for knowing she had lost her two best friends, or maybe it was something else. I just knew it bothered me to see her like that. "Tell me and I'll decide if it's silly."

She sniffed again. "It's Claire."

I stiffened. "What do you mean?"

"I like Claire, all right," she confessed, taking me aback. Wait ... Harper liked Claire? For real? "But I heard earlier this afternoon when Tanner asked her out. I guess they are dating now." A thick tear rolled down her cheek. "And I've got no chance."

I sat down beside her. "Ah, Harper, don't feel so bad." I honestly didn't know what to say to her. I didn't want to tell her Tanner was a douche and it probably wouldn't last, because I didn't want to give her hope. What if Claire's touch was magical and she easily changed Tanner and he became the nicest guy around? But I didn't want to tell her to forget about Claire, not yet. First, because it was too soon. Two, because if I could choose for Claire, I would choose Harper. I patted her arm. "It's going to be okay."

Harper rested her head on my shoulder. "You think so?"

I let out a sigh and decided to be honest, "I hope so."

Hope. That was the thread that led my life. I hoped I would

live to the end of the day. I hoped I would get good grades. I hoped I didn't embarrass my mother anymore. I hoped Ava and I didn't cross paths. I hoped I forgot about Rey soon. I hoped Thierry turned out to be an amazing guy and I fell in love with him.

Moreover, I hoped my father, the supreme demon, forgot I existed and never came for me.

14

AVOIDING ERIN FOR THE LAST COUPLE OF WEEKS HAD BEEN WAY too hard, especially after our time together forging her Dawnblade. A week ago, I found out Thierry had come to campus to work with her on the ball's preparations. It had taken every ounce of my will not to go spy on them. To not interrupt them again before Thierry kissed not only her hand, but also her lips.

Trying to get Erin out of my mind for a change, I headed out of the academy to meet up with an old friend.

I drove past West Hill, onto an isolated road that led to a small ranch at the mountain's base. Here the snow still covered most of the ground, and the road leading to the main house was thick with ice. I drove slowly and parked my car beside the beat up truck in front of the barn.

With her long brown hair tied in a loose braid, Vaira stomped out the house, stopped by the edge of the porch, and pointed her finger at me. "No, I don't want to see you right now. Get off my property."

Did I mention she was a friend? Yeah, that was a fucking lie. We were more like acquaintances and not good ones.

About a hundred years ago, Asmodeus sent me on a contract-dealing mission for Zeltov, another prince of the underworld. He said a woman in her early thirties was about to lose her mother and would do anything to avoid that grim fate. So, I went to her and offered a contract—if the woman gave her soul to Zeltov, her mother would be saved. The woman didn't hesitate.

But there was a catch. Like me, the woman was half-demon, daughter of the prince she had sold her soul to. And because of that, the prince was able to bind her to him indefinitely. Like mine, her contract didn't have an end date. Like my story, her mother lived for a long time, but in the end died and left her alone.

However, I was able to get rid of my contract when Asmodeus died. I was still immortal and powerful, and I would always be a half-demon, but my ties to the underworld had been severed.

Vaira's were still intact.

I had always felt bad for brokering her contract and dooming her to such a horrible fate. Because of it, I tried checking on her occasionally, but she always pushed me away. Truth was, she hated me for what I had done.

I couldn't blame her.

"I came with an offer," I said, knowing that didn't sound good at all.

Vaira put her hands on her waist. "Are you fucking serious?"

"Just hear me out." I took a couple of steps toward her, soaking my boots and feet into the snow. "Randall is creating a unit of half-demons. He says he wants to show the demon hunters that not all half-demons are evil. He wants to introduce them to the demon hunter society."

She scoffed. "Randall is crazy."

"He's also powerful," I said. "A few months ago, he killed my father and I was freed of my contract."

Her eyes widened. "Randall killed Prince Asmodeus? I hadn't heard that."

"You live buried in this ranch." I gestured around. Besides the main house and the barn, there was only snow and trees covered with snow. "How can you hear anything out here?"

"Get to the point, Rey," she warned, her eyes narrowed.

"If you join us, you might end up on Randall's good side. Then if you ask, he might kill Prince Zeltov for you." I paused for effect. "And you would be free of your contract."

She hesitated. "I don't trust Randall."

"Neither do I." But unfortunately, I had no choice here. I didn't tell her about my deal with Randall, because she might think she would have to do one with him too. Which was a possibility, of course. "But if his intentions are true, this is a good opportunity for us."

She frowned, considering. "If I join this group, my main goal will be to take my father down and gain my freedom."

I nodded once. "I understand."

Vaira let out a long breath. "All right. I'll join your fucking half-demon unit. But be warned, Rey. I better not regret this."

"You won't," I told her, though I couldn't guarantee anything.

Satisfied with my work, Vaira and I shook hands, and I gave her one of the amulets Randall had asked the half-demons to wear. After, I went back to the academy satisfied by making progress with my mission.

* * *

MY MIND WAS BLISSFULLY BLANK AS I DROVE PAST THE ACADEMY front gates and parked my car in its usual spot in the underground garage. But as I started walking toward the Snapdragon building, I thought of crossing by the Gardenia building, where Erin probably was at this time.

I halted before I left the garage and took a deep breath, forcing my fucking mind to focus on anything else.

The squeal of tires echoed through the garage, and I turned as a car zoomed toward me.

What the fuck?

The car didn't stop. I jumped to the side to avoid being hit.

Then, the car stopped and Zachary hopped out. "You," he snarled.

"What the fuck?" I asked, feeling my blood warming with rage. "Were you trying to run me over?"

Zachary didn't answer. He just came at me and landed a punch on my chin.

My head barely moved with the impact, but pain spread through my jaw, my cheeks, and my neck.

The motherfucker.

He pulled his arm back to punch me again. I summoned a wall of darkfire that enveloped him, constricting his movements.

"Let me go!" he yelled.

Why didn't he use his powers to counter my darkfire wall and get free? He had thrown darkfire at Erin when we went to visit him the first time, which meant, he knew about his powers. But perhaps he didn't know how to use them? I thought of Erin and how she too didn't know how to summon and control darkfire at first.

Fuck. This entire half-demon army would be untrained, and guess who Randall would put in charge of their training?

"I don't like being hit without a reason." I touched my chin, checking that nothing was broken. "Actually, I don't like being hit, period."

"It's all because of you!" he yelled, struggling against the darkfire. "You and Erin! I'll make you two pay!"

I frowned. Until now, I was irritated. The moment he mentioned Erin, I became murderous. "What the fuck happened?"

"What do you think? Susan found out I'm a half-demon. She said she was disgusted and scared of me, and she left me." His shoulders dropped, as if he was tired of fighting. "She kicked me out."

"How?"

"I was doing some work the headmaster ordered me to do," he said, as if that made sense. "And she saw me."

"Wait? What work?" I asked, confused. Randall had assigned him a task? When? Why? And why didn't I know about that?

Zachary let out a scream. In his rage, he finally broke through the darkfire wall and summoned a bolt in his hand. He threw it at me.

I raised my hand and caught his bolt, as if it had been a tennis ball he had thrown my way. "I don't want to fight with you, Zachary." I closed my hand and the bolt disappeared. "Just tell me what Randall ordered you to do?"

He jutted his finger in my face. "I'll make you pay. You and Erin. You'll both pay for what you did to me."

Blind with rage, Zachary slipped inside his car and drove away.

I shook my head, weary and wary. I was so fucking tired of fighting, arguing, scheming, lying, deceiving ... I had been living like this for almost a thousand years, and sometimes I felt like it would never end, no matter what I did.

Letting out a long breath, I forced my feet to move, but not to my room in the Snapdragon building, but to the Aster building, where I would check the security on campus before heading to bed. Having a deranged half-demon loose on campus who was intent on getting revenge on Erin and me had put me on edge.

15

ERIN

I was sweating cold when I woke up early in the morning from a nightmare—another one with Brianne and Cindy.

Why did I keep having these dreams? Was there a meaning to them? Maybe if I could save them in these dreams, they would leave me alone?

Sure I wouldn't be able to fall back asleep, I got up, got dressed, and headed to the Hyacinth building over an hour earlier than usual. By the time my mother walked into the classroom, I was already dripping in sweat, but this time from training.

Martha didn't say anything as we started the usual practice, but I noticed she wanted to.

During one of our water breaks, she stood before me. "I can see something is bothering you. What is it?"

I frowned. She was my mother. She was training me because she wanted me to be the best of the best, so I could defend myself and keep myself alive. She had sacrificed a lot for me.

And yet ... I didn't really know her, and I didn't trust her.

Well, in some way, I did, but not enough to confide in her, to tell her about my problems and my recurring nightmares.

"Nothing," I said.

My mother's brows curled down. "Why don't you want to tell me?"

I shrugged. "There's nothing to tell."

"You're lying." Her frown deepened. "You don't trust me."

Shit, she sounded hurt. "I-it's not—"

"You hesitated," she said. "That means you really don't trust me."

"That's not it," I whispered, not sure what to say to her.

"You've been hiding things from me lately," she pointed out. "You know I'm here to help you. All I do is to help you, to protect you. Even when it seems wrong or misguided, it's all for you."

"You barely know me," I whispered.

"You're my daughter. That's all I need to know."

Was there love in her words? In her actions? Or was it just because we shared the same blood? Maybe it wasn't because she was scared for me, but scared of what I could do. After all, I was a demonic princess. If I wanted, I could probably raise my own legion of demons and become as evil as King Brikan.

"You're doing this because you feel bad," I said, inhaling the air deep in my lungs. "Because you feel guilty for bringing a child like me into the world."

"Don't be ridiculous!" she snapped, her eyes fuming. "I'm training you to protect you."

"Protect me from whom?"

"Erin, do you hear yourself? Why did you change the subject? All I wanted was for you to trust me and tell me what's wrong."

Disappointed with the truth, I crossed my arms. "You're practically a stranger. How can I trust a stranger?"

My mother's eyes bugged, and for the first time since I met her, she genuinely seemed shocked. "Fine." She picked up her towel. "If you don't trust me enough to tell me what is going on, and if you think I'm training you because you're a threat, then we're done here." She lifted her chin, proud. "I don't see any point in continuing these training sessions."

I stared at her, shocked. "What does that have to do with anything?"

"Don't wake up early tomorrow." She turned and started walking away.

"You said that before," I said louder, remembering a few weeks ago when we stopped training, but she came after me and dragged me back to the gym a few days later.

"It won't happen this time."

She walked out the classroom and I stared at the doorway, confused. What the hell? Was she my mother or a fifteen-year-old? She seemed hurt by my accusation that she was training me to protect others from me, but what did she expect? My mind was wild, and when there were so many secrets around me, I could only take a guess. If I was wrong, she should have stayed and proved it to me.

Well, fine by me. If quitting our training sessions meant I could sleep for a couple more hours each morning, great.

That was if the nightmares left me alone.

With time to spare, I went back to the Gardenia building. I didn't have time to go back to sleep, not that I could even if I wanted to, so I took a shower, put on my uniform, and checked my books and notebooks for the day.

The first class was demon history, which I really liked, but still felt overwhelming. There was so much I didn't know and would probably never know. The demon hunters and demon history were as old as the world itself. There were too many wars and events; it would be impossible to know them all.

Curious about our next lesson, I flipped through the pages for the next chapter. It was about the legends that spurred several wars. I skimmed through the titles of the legends until one of them caught my attention.

The Demon Kissed Queens.

I sat down on my desk and started reading the legend.

It told the story of three half-sisters, daughters of a powerful demon, whose destinies were marked in stone.

Wait.

Three half-sisters.

Daughters of a powerful demon.

This was about me, Brianne, and Cindy. It had to be.

I flipped the pages, trying to read more, but there was nothing else.

Shit, it couldn't be.

With my book under my arm, I went to the library. It was mostly empty, as everyone was either just waking up or having breakfast before class.

I sat down in front of one of the computers by the entrance and typed "Demon Kissed Queens" in the search box. No books showed up.

Frowning, I tried "King Brikan legends" and a long list of books appeared on the screen. I read their titles and marked down the ones that seemed interesting. Then, I went around the library, grabbing many of them, and sat down at a corner table where I could research in peace.

First, I opened all the books to the index pages and tried finding the legend's title. It took me a few books, but finally, I found a thin book with the legend.

But it wasn't any more helpful than the demon history textbook.

All it said was that one day there would be three half-sisters, daughters of the Supreme Demon, who were destined to kill the king of the underworld, and change the supernatural world forever.

The next paragraph dismissed this legend, saying it was a rumor, considered to be more like an old wives' tale, started by demons who supposedly were against Brikan. It was regarded as a fanciful story.

But it wasn't. Deep in my gut, I knew it wasn't.

Brianne, Cindy, and I were the daughters of the Supreme Demon.

Were we meant to kill him? What happened when there was only one daughter left? Was the legend just the rumor the book claimed it to be?

For months, I had thought the king wanted to take me to the underworld to have me with him, so we could rule together, like a twisted family, or something like that. But no ... he probably wanted to kill me so I couldn't kill him.

But how? He was the king of the underworld! There was no way I could kill him. Not even with my new, fancy Dawnblade.

I searched through the other books but only found one other mention of this legend, and this entry had even less info.

I need to know more, damn it. What I needed was to find the real legend, or prophecy, and the exact wording. But where?

I glanced to the closed off section of the library. It was a simple door in the back that led to a room like this one, but with books that were forbidden to the students.

Rey had access to that room.

I could ask him ...

No, I couldn't. Didn't I argue with him to let me go? Then I couldn't hold on to him either. I had to figure out this stuff by myself.

"There you are," Claire said as she walked to me. "I was looking everywhere for you."

I frowned. "Shit, am I going to be late for class?"

She stopped in front of my table. "Erin, you already missed demon history."

"What?" I glanced at my watch. It was already mid-morning. "Holy shit!"

She sat down beside me and turned her attention to the stack of books on my table. "What are you researching?"

I smiled, realizing that maybe I didn't need to figure this out by myself. I had my best friend to help, and thankfully, she loved researching and studying.

I showed her the entry I had found about the Demon Kissed Queens, and how I thought it was about Brianne, Cindy, and me. "It makes sense, right?"

Slowly, she nodded. "It does." She turned the book to herself and read the entry again. "Did you find anything else?"

I let out a long sigh. "Nope."

Claire shot me a determined look. "Don't worry. I'm here now and I won't give up until I find something."

My smile came back as my chest warmed. My best friend was really the best.

16

REY

AFTER SEARCHING FOR ZACHARY SINCE LAST NIGHT AND NOT finding him anywhere, I debated all morning what to do. I could simply keep an eye out and remain quiet about this.

Or I could tell Erin that Zachary had a crazy outburst and had promised to make us pay.

The best choice was to tell her, so she could prepare in case I wasn't nearby to help, but that meant I had to find her. I had to go to her. I had to talk to her, to look at her, to be near her.

And that was all I was avoiding so fucking hard.

Knowing it was the right thing to do, I dragged my feet all over the academy until I found her inside the library in the Iris building with Claire. They were seated at a small table stacked high with books.

I halted beside the table. "Hm, Erin, can I talk to you?"

She lifted her golden eyes from the book she was reading and immediately frowned. "What about?"

I pressed my lips tight.

"Hm ..." Claire stood up. "I'm going to get more books."

She dashed between the shelves of books and I was grateful for it.

Erin returned her gaze to the book in her arms.

"Last night, Zachary threatened me," I started. "Well, he threatened both of us."

That got her attention and she looked at me again. "Why would he do that?"

"His wife found out he's a half-demon," I said, my voice lower so no one else would listen. "He blames us for that."

"He should blame you. You're the one who blackmailed him."

Would she ever forget about that? "All right, I promise not to blackmail anyone anymore. Are you happy now?"

Her golden eyes burned into mine. "Not in the slightest."

What did that fucking mean? That comment was loaded and I wasn't going to take the bait.

"Anyway, now you know." I took a step back. "Be careful."

I turned to leave but stopped when I saw Sandra, one of the school's staff, coming our way, a small black envelope in her hand. Without saying a word, she handed me the envelope and left.

Frowning, I opened the envelope, pulled out the white paper, and read the note.

Come to my office. Bring Erin.

—R.

I lowered the envelope and paper and glanced at Erin. She was looking at me, a knot between her brows.

"What is it?" she asked. I handed the note to her. She read it. "Shit."

"I had more colorful words in mind, but, yeah, that too." I let out a heavy exhale. "Let's go."

Erin took her time getting up, putting her things away

and warning Claire that she had to go see Randall. I wasn't so sure it was good for Claire to know so much about what we were doing, but I doubted Erin would stop telling her if I said something. In fact, I was sure it would have the opposite effect.

We walked side by side, but in silence. In my mind, I tried initiating conversations, but I always gave up. It would only make things worse.

Outside of Randall's office, we heard shouting. Erin and I exchanged a wary look. She probably wondered the same thing I did: Should we step back so we didn't hear it, or should we walk in before the shouting became something worse?

But three seconds later, the door burst open and Professor Crimson stomped out of the office. He sneered at Erin and me before going on his way.

I knocked on the door once and peeked inside. "Everything okay?"

Watching out the window overlooking the Blackthorn tree, Randall waved us in. "Just the same nonsense." Erin and I entered the room and closed the door. Sighing, Randall turned to us. "He thinks that yelling at me and being rude will suddenly make him the headmaster." Randall shook his head.

I frowned. Though I doubted Erin knew, it was no secret that Professor Crimson didn't like Randall and coveted the headmaster's seat. I never understood why since Randall was fucking immortal. The only way to have his seat was to kill him.

"Did you call?" Erin asked, her tone still stiff.

"Yes, indeed." He sat down, then gestured to the two chairs in front of his desk. Erin and I took the seats. "I have a new assignment for you. A group of half-demons, living in a small settlement, was located a few hours from here. I want you to go there and convince them to join the Black Knight Unit."

I understood if he asked that of me, but Erin? She wasn't trained as I was. She wasn't as strong as I was. She wasn't as vicious as I was. "Isn't that dangerous?" I asked, hoping he got my meaning.

His eyes flicked to Erin. Yup, he knew what I meant. "Yes. I actually heard the settlement doesn't take kindly to outsiders, so it should be risky and dangerous, but I believe you two might be an exception."

"How?" I asked, not following.

Randall shrugged. "Because I believe in your abilities."

"Are we going today?" Erin asked, as if she was eager to go.

"You still have classes to attend this afternoon," Randall said. "Why don't you go this weekend? That should work better."

With that decided, Randall dismissed us.

Erin and I left his office and headed out of the Aster building. She headed back to the library and I planned to walk away from her, but then she sped her steps as if running somewhere. Then I saw it.

Seated on a bench in the courtyard, Claire shrank into herself while Tanner hovered over her, his body tense and his hands balled into fists.

I stopped and watched for a moment.

"You're stupid!" Tanner yelled. "That's what you are."

Erin halted beside him and pushed him back. "What the hell do you think you're doing?"

"This is none of your business!" Tanner yelled at her.

Oh, my blood started to fucking boil.

"Of course it is my business," Erin snapped. "If you hurt my best friend, it's my damn business."

Tanner let out a mean chuckle. "I'm not hurting her. I was just telling the truth."

Erin's shoulders tensed. "Get out of here before I kick your ass."

Tanner took a step closer to her and faced her down. "I would like to see you try."

"I will do it," Erin warned.

Gritting his teeth, Tanner pulled his hand back—

I used my demon speed and suddenly appeared beside them and gripped Tanner's arm. "I don't think so." I pushed him back and he stumbled several feet back.

Eyes wide, Tanner stared at me. "Where did you come from?"

"That doesn't matter," I said, knowing I had been careless. I doubted anyone had really seen me, but somebody could have. "Now get out of here before I break your fucking face."

Tanner shifted his weight for about four seconds before throwing a death glare at Claire and running away.

Beside me, Erin sat down with Claire and embraced her friend, who now cried openly. "It's okay now." She rubbed Claire's back up and down. "He's a jerk and doesn't deserve you. You're better off without him."

At that, Claire pulled back and stared at Erin as if she had gone crazy. "Better off without him? No, I need him. I love him." She sniffed, trying to contain the tears. "And I know he loves me too."

"You call that love?" The words flew from my fucking mouth.

Claire's cheek reddened, matching her swollen eyes. "It's just ... he gets mad from time to time, but it's not his fault."

Erin's brows slammed down. "And whose fault is it?"

"Me," Claire whispered. "You heard him. I'm stupid, so I say some stupid things sometimes."

"What?" Erin shrieked. "That's not true, Claire. Are you listening to yourself? That's nonsense!"

"I agree with Erin," I said, trying to help. "He's a douchebag and you can't believe anything Tanner says."

Surprising us, Claire shot to her feet and glared at us. "Obviously, you two don't get it."

She stomped away.

Erin stood. "Claire?" She turned to me. "What the hell was that?" She glanced back at her friend. "I should go after her."

I shook my head. "Arguing with her right now won't help. She needs time to cool down."

Erin sighed and slumped down on the cold bench. "You're right."

I sat down beside her. "I feel like going after Tanner and beating the fuck out of him, so I can't imagine how you feel right now."

"Beating the fuck out of him would be only half of it," she said, her voice low. "Claire is such a sweet person. I don't know how the two of them got mixed up."

"Me neither."

Slowly, she turned her eyes to me. Even under the dark gray sky, her golden eyes shone as bright as the sun. "What about us? Shouldn't we stop getting mixed up?"

"I'm trying, but things keep pulling us together," I confessed. Maybe if I was mean to her again, or made it clear I really wanted to stay away from her, she would do her part.

But when Randall gave us assignments like that, how could we?

"Don't you think that means something?" she asked, her voice holding a hopeful tone.

Feeling like such a fucking liar, I shook my head. "Don't read too much into it, Erin. It means nothing."

"I'm not so sure about that," she whispered.

Holy fuck, when she pushed like that ... it was so hard to hold on. To pull back. To ignore her.

It was fucking impossible to ignore her. All I could *try* to do was pretend. I pretended I ignored her.

Donning my jerk hat, I shot to my feet. "If you're going to keep talking about that, I'm leaving."

Erin lifted her face, looking up at me, a sad shine in her eyes. "Good night, Rey."

Wow.

Why did having her practically telling me to go hurt so fucking much? Perhaps deep inside, I was still hoping she would hold on to me.

That was terribly twisted.

"Night," I said before walking away from her.

17

OLD HABITS DIED HARD. I DIDN'T HAVE TRAINING WITH MY mother in the morning, but I still woke up at the crack of dawn.

I freaking hated it.

At first, I tried to go back to sleep, but when I couldn't, I got up, got dressed, and went to train by myself. Sometimes I did some exercises in the martial arts classroom in the Hyacinth building, sometimes I went to the gym for some weight lifting, and sometimes I went to the track behind the building to run.

But this morning, I didn't feel like working out. So, I headed to the library instead. Claire and I had been researching the Demon Kissed Queens legend, but hadn't found anything useful yet. Claire had even searched her father's books at their townhouse at the Dahlia Villa, but so far she had found nothing.

Until today.

I was buried underneath a tall pile of books when Claire

came running into the library, holding what looked like a thick ledger.

"I found it," she said, out of breath.

I glanced up at her, glad to see she looked okay. Right after her fight with Tanner, she avoided me. Once she let me approach her, she snapped at me if I brought up his name. Now, I did my best to keep that subject bottled up inside, but I swore ... if that guy was mean to her again, I would beat him up and do all I could to keep Claire away from him. Even if she hated me for it after.

"What did you find?" I asked.

She took the seat beside me and opened the ledger on her lap. "I found this among my father's book. It's a catalog of all the books in the academy."

"You mean, the ones in the library?"

She shook her head. "No, I mean in the academy. It lists books in the library, the classrooms, the infirmary, and personal collections, like my father's, your mother's, and even the headmaster's!"

I stared at her. "But ... why?"

She shrugged. "I don't know. It's handwritten, so I'm guessing my father is trying to keep tabs on all the books around campus. I would say the list is incomplete, but the book we want is mentioned here."

I gasped. "You mean, a book about the Demon Kissed Queen legend?"

"Yes!" She flipped to a specific page and showed me the list. "Here. See? The Demon Kissed Queens book. It's supposed to be in this library, on shelf H1."

I frowned. Shelf H1? Where was that? I walked around the shelves in the library, looking for it, but I only found shelves that went from A to Z. Once that was done, the shelves started again, but with AA, BB, CC ...

I halted in front of the door to the restricted section. I had been there before with Rey, but I hadn't paid attention to the shelves' numbering. But where else could it be?

Claire halted by my side. "You think it's in there?"

"That's my guess," I said.

"I doubt we'll be allowed inside, though."

I glanced at the lock on the door. "Think we can break in?"

She turned wide eyes at me. "What? Right now?"

"No, at night, when the library is closed."

She sucked in a sharp breath. "You want to sneak into the library and break into the restricted section?" Slowly, her lips stretched into a smile. "I'm in."

I chuckled. "As if you had a choice."

* * *

Claire and I went on with our regular schedule: classes, break for lunch, more classes. Then she disappeared while I headed to the gym—I bet she went to see Tanner. Later, we got together for dinner, and now we waited in the media room until it was late, and everyone was sleeping.

It was almost midnight when we finally made our way to the library. At least I didn't have to wake up early for training tomorrow morning.

We stuck to the shadows along the building as much as we could, and we listened for any kind of noise, so we wouldn't run into a guard patrolling the pathways. I still had my pass from my mother, but I didn't want to use it tonight.

Surprisingly, the library was unlocked. Well, when there were only students around, why not keep the one place they might study open twenty-four-seven, right? Still, it seemed odd to me.

In the dark, we made our way to the back.

We halted before the door to the restricted section.

"So, what now?" I asked Claire in a low voice. "Do we just break the lock?" As if that would be easy. Maybe if I used my magic ...

"Here." Claire fished out a card from her pocket. "It's my father's access card."

Claire had stolen the card from her father. That was quite shocking. "How did you get it?"

"I stopped by the house between classes," she said. And I had imagined she had ditched me to spend time with her douche boyfriend. "All I need to do is put it back in place early tomorrow morning."

I smiled at her. "You're a genius."

She shrugged. "Not really."

"Okay, miss genius, then open the freaking door."

Claire swiped the card into the card reader. A green light appeared along with a faint click. She turned the door, and pushed.

The door opened.

We rushed inside and closed the door. Not wanting to turn on the lights in the room, I used the flashlight Claire had brought—she was always ready—and searched for the H1 shelf.

Here, all the shelves were labeled with one letter and one number, instead of one or two letters, so it was easy to follow the alphabet and find the H1 shelf.

Then Claire told me the book number. I started reading the labels on the spine, searching for the book.

But when I got to it, there was an empty space on the shelf. My stomach dropped. "It's missing," I whispered, pulling back. I stared at the empty space, as if I could conjure the book back. "It can't be."

"No," Claire said with a gasp. Then she stiffened. "It has to be around here somewhere." She went back to the table in the middle of the room. "You know when you get a book and leave it on the table, and then later the librarian has to return it to its place? Maybe the book is somewhere, ready to be placed back on the shelf."

She went from table to table, and despite thinking we wouldn't find anything, I searched with her. We looked over all the tables and carts and desks. The book was nowhere to be seen.

"Someone must have taken it." I said what had been on my mind since we first saw the book was missing.

"Wait." Claire turned to the desk with computers along the wall. She sat down in front of one, fired it up, and searched for the book. "It's showing here as the book is still available. Which means—"

"The book was not only taken, but it was taken without permission."

Claire glanced at me. "But who? Who could have wanted this book?"

I shrugged. "I don't have a clue." Could anyone else know about this legend, or believe it was true, like we did? I hadn't even told Rey about it. No one should have known about this.

Unless it was a super curious person who liked studying legends. But that was a huge coincidence.

Claire stood. "What do we do now?"

"Right now? Go back to bed. It's late and we probably won't solve this tonight." It was true, but I was sure I wouldn't be able to sleep, not when I knew there was a book like that and it was missing.

I would wonder who took it all night long.

Defeated, Claire and I started back to the front area of the library. We were lost in thought and almost jumped out of our skin when a low growl started.

Claire grabbed my arm. "What's that?"

Suddenly, a shadow jumped from behind the shelves.

"A demon!" Claire yelped, taking cover behind me.

In the dark, I tried taking it in, to determine how to best kill it, while taking a few steps back. It was tall and lean like a human, with pitch black skin, a skeletal face, and horns on their bald heads. Their eyes sockets were hollow, and their mouth was a long slit from side to side, filled with sharp fangs.

"A darkelth," I muttered.

Claire whimpered. "Summon your Dawnblade. Kill it!"

The demon let out another growl.

Then it pounced.

I pushed Claire aside and out of the way, and I called for my Dawnblade. I pulled it back, ready to drive it in the creature's chest, when the tip of another sword pierced it. The demon gurgled, snapping its teeth at me. The blade was withdrawn and the demon folded forward at my feet.

I dropped my arm and dismissed my Dawnblade.

Tanner lowered his Dawnblade. He stared at the demon for a moment, before looking at me. "Are you okay?" I nodded, completely confused. He turned to Claire, who was cowering beside a desk. "Hey, Claire, it's me."

Claire opened her eyes and let out a long sigh. "Oh, Tanner." She flung herself in his arms.

Letting go of his Dawnblade, Tanner caught her and squeezed her tight. "I've got you."

"I'm so glad you came," she said, still holding to him. "This demon would have hurt us."

"Hmm," I muttered. One, nope, the demon wouldn't have hurt us. Well, it might have, but I would have fought it and I was confident in my skills now. I would probably never be as fantastic as Rey, but I could kill that kind of demon. I was sure. Two ... "Tanner, what are you doing here?"

"Oh." He pushed Claire to the side, so he embraced her with one arm and turned his grin at me. Had he already forgotten about our argument the other day? "I was working on my homework and felt restless, so I went for a walk to clear my mind and wear me out. I was walking by the library when I thought I saw movement inside. I'm glad I decided to check it out."

"You're my hero," Claire said, smiling wide.

Holy shit, she sounded so nauseating even to me.

Then his grin was gone. "You two shouldn't be lurking around the academy so late at night. Come on. I'll escort you back to the dorms."

Slipping his hand into Claire's, Tanner took the lead and headed out of the library.

I stayed back for a few seconds, trying to wrap my mind around what had just happened. Why would a demon be lurking around the library like that? Why would Tanner show up at the library in the middle of the night? And who the hell had taken the book?

Of course, the first thing that came to mind was that Tanner had taken the book, and he somehow had brought that demon to kill it in front of Claire and gain even more of her favor. But that didn't make sense. And even if it did, it was too obvious.

Something wasn't right here.

With a feeling that bugged me to no end, I followed Tanner and Claire to the dorms.

18

REY

I talked to Randall about letting Erin out of the next mission. Not because I didn't think she could handle going to this half-demon settlement with me, but because it meant I had to spend more time alone with her.

Each time I spent time with her, my resolution to stay away from her shook.

Worse than that, the fucking weather. It was already the end of February, and it had snowed two days ago, dumping a fresh coat of white shit all over the campus. I had lived all over the world for the past thousand years, and though I didn't like extreme heat either, I would take a place with a scorching sun over snow any day.

This Saturday wasn't any better. The sun was out, but the day was damn cold. Wearing a thick, black coat and beanie, Erin met me in the underground garage.

She nodded her chin at me as if saying hi and slipped inside my car.

Oh-kay.

I tried staying quiet and let her deal with her bad mood

alone, but the tension inside my car as we drove to the settlement was too much to bear. That, and her sweet rose scent tickling my nose drove me to the edge.

Finally, I gave in. "What's wrong?"

Eyes out the window, Erin scoffed. "It would be better to ask what's *not* wrong."

"Then tell me the latest problem," I insisted, even though I knew I shouldn't.

She turned her golden eyes to me. "All right."

Then, she launched into a tale about how she and Claire had been researching King Brikan since she found out she was his daughter. They found a legend titled Demon Kissed Queens—about three half-siblings who would defeat the underworld together. She had been trying to find more about that legend ever since, but when she finally found a book that apparently could contain all the answers, the book was gone.

"When Claire and I were leaving the library, a darkelth demon attacked us, and—"

"Wait." I almost jerked the car off the road. "A darkelth demon was on school grounds? And you didn't tell me? You know I'm still working with the campus security, right?"

"Right," she said, deadpan. I glanced at her and found her expression as cold as her voice. She hadn't told me on purpose. That was what I got for pushing her away.

Fuck.

"What happened then?" I asked through gritted teeth.

"I was about to kill the demon when Tanner showed up. He killed the demon and was hailed a hero by Claire."

"Don't tell me she didn't think it was suspicious for him to be there in the middle of the night, when the book was missing, and there was a fucking demon on the loose?"

"Exactly," she said, exasperated. "I tried talking to her

about it today, and she cut me off, saying that Tanner would never do that."

I scoffed. "Right."

"So you agree with me. He's suspicious, right? I have to investigate him."

I didn't like that. "Erin, I understand your need to find out more about what's happening, but you should be careful. If Tanner is behind all that, then he's not a good guy."

Her face hardened again. "You've made it perfectly clear you don't care about me, Rey, so please, don't concern yourself with my safety." Like a petulant child, she crossed her arms and faced straight ahead.

I gripped the wheel of my car, until my knuckles became white, trying hard to contain all the words stuck in my throat. If I had a choice, I would never leave her side. I would be there with her, training her. I would be looking for this fucking legend with her, and I would be there when the demon attacked to protect her.

But it couldn't be that way. In my mind, I sounded like a fucking broken record, but it was true. I knew Erin was in danger just for being who she was, but with me around her? It was double the danger. And if Randall found out about my feelings for her? He would manipulate me even more. He might even manipulate her. I couldn't allow it.

She was better off without me and my tainted life.

The tension and animosity remained heavy the rest of the way to the half-demon settlement. Soon, I veered my car off the road, and parked when we had nowhere else to go.

Erin hopped out of the car and hugged herself against the chilly wind. "What now?"

"According to Randall, we head this way and should find it in less than a mile."

"Fantastic," she said, her tone sarcastic.

She trudged forward and I was glad she was wearing snow boots. At least her feet wouldn't get cold.

What the fuck was I thinking?

Keeping a safe distance from Erin, I marched through the forest, sinking my boots in the snow. At least here, the naked branches of the trees were so close that the snow wasn't deep.

It was easy to spot when we got close to the settlement. The snow had been shoveled away, first as paths, then it spread as a small clearing appeared. A big bonfire sat in the center of the clearing, many tree trunks lined around it, serving as benches. Beyond it, small cottages lined the trees.

And between it all—talking, sitting, walking—were the half-demons.

Noticing our presence, they all froze and looked at us.

"Come on," I whispered to Erin, walking into the clearing.

A man stood up from one of the trunks and took a few steps toward us. He was of average height, with dark skin and messy black hair. With the opulent fur coat around his shoulders, he looked big, stocky, but I could be mistaken.

"Who are you?" he asked, halting a few feet from us.

I halted too, and a moment later, Erin stopped half a foot behind me. "I'm Rey Lowe, and this is Erin Delman." Technically, Erin was now Belmont. Delman had been a decoy her aunt had created to hide their real name. But no one knew about that yet, so we kept using her fake last name. "We're half-demons like you."

The man wrinkled his nose, and the nasty scar cutting from the corner of his lips to his ear became more noticeable. "Are you here seeking refuge? How did you find us?"

"Actually, we're here to talk to you and make you an offer," I said, aiming for a stable and diplomatic tone. To this man, I was a twenty-two-year-old half-demon, while he was at least ten years older than that. He probably thought he could intimidate me.

He tilted his head. "An offer?"

"We're not only half-demons but also half demon hunter," I told him. "We study at the Blackthorn Hunters Academy. Our headmaster, Randall Boucher, knows about our heritage and he doesn't mind. In fact, he would like to offer—"

The man scoffed loudly. "I don't like Randall."

Of course he had heard of Randall. Who in the supernatural world hadn't? "I understand your sentiment, but you should hear the offer. Maybe it'll change your mind."

"Excuse me. What's your name?" Erin asked, stepping forward, slightly in front of me. Her beautiful face was passive and her eyes twinkled bright.

The man regarded her with a scowl. "I'm Daermarn."

"Hi, Daermarn, I'm Erin Delman," she started with a faint smile. "I'll be honest, I'm new to this whole thing. It was only about seven months ago that I found out I'm half demon hunter, and a half-demon. Even so, I can see this is an opportunity. Headmaster Randall trusts Rey and me, despite our heritage, which shows he cares about us. What the headmaster wants is to integrate half-demons into our society. It's a chance for every half-demon to come out into the light and stop hiding."

Daermarn watched Erin with narrowed eyes. "That is quite interesting, but what do we have to do in return?"

"Join the headmaster's half-demon group, the Black Knight Unit, and work with us toward this goal," Erin said, sounding like a saleswoman. I had to hand it to her. Her words were compelling and I could see Daermarn relaxing.

"That all sounds like a dream come true, but like I said, I

don't trust Randall," Daermarn said. "I'll have to ask you to leave."

Erin's eyes rounded.

On instinct, I channeled my magic, ready to put up a fight if they tried to hurt us.

"Stop being such a jackass, Daer."

I turned to the new voice. Vaira walked into the clearing. "What are you doing here?" I asked, confused.

Ignoring me, Vaira walked to Daermarn. When she was in arm's reach, he clasped his hand around her waist and tugged her close. "I'm not being a jackass," Daermarn said, his voice softer.

Wait ...

Vaira glanced at me. "I'm here because Daermarn is my partner." Then she looked at him. "I've talked to Randall and, I can't believe I'm saying this, but I believe him. He wants to help us."

"You believe him?" Daermarn asked incredulously.

Vaira nodded. "I do. And you should too."

He frowned at her but didn't say anything. It was as if they could communicate through their eyes, their minds. Were they soulmates?

I glanced at Erin, who stood stiffened by my side, waiting for an answer. My soulmate was by my side, and she didn't even know it.

"All right," Daermarn said, capturing my attention. "I'm not taking part in this, but I'll let my people decide for themselves. If they want to join this Black Knight Unit, I won't stop them. However, I want immunity for our town."

I frowned. It wasn't in my power to grant him immunity. "I'll talk to Randall and make the request."

Daermarn nodded. "Sounds good enough. For now."

With Vaira on his arm, Daermarn turned to his people, who had all gathered around the bonfire while we talked, and he explained the offer. Vaira chipped in, saying she was a part of the Black Knight Unit and she believed in it.

In the end, half of the settlement agreed to join. Vaira went around, collecting their names on a list for us and delivering the silver coin amulets. Then, a while later, she handed the list to me.

"Thank you," I said to her as I took the list.

She narrowed her eyes at me. "This wasn't free, Rey. You owe me a favor now."

Fuck. "I should have known."

She nodded at Erin, then walked back to the rest of the group.

Clearly dismissed, Erin and I made our way back to the car. During the drive to the academy, Erin remained silent, lost in her thoughts. Mine swam over words of what to say. I wanted to tell her she had done well, that she had swayed Daermarn, and even if Vaira hadn't come along, she would have persuaded him to allow his people to join our cause.

But I didn't. Instead, I held my fucking tongue, knowing that the more I told her, the more I talked to her, the worse it would be.

For her and for me.

As instructed, we went directly to Randall's office at the Aster building once we got back to the academy.

Randall was waiting for us, eager to hear about the deal. "So?" he asked, his fingers steepled over his desk.

"We were able to get half the settlement to join the Black Knight Unit," I told him. Erin and I stood on the other side of his desk, like two rigid statues.

"Only half?" His tone wasn't happy.

"Unfortunately, the leader Daermarn doesn't trust you, but he allowed his people to choose. Half of his people sign up for the unit," Erin said, once more sounding calm and wise. "Unless he gives in, I doubt there will be any way to convince them all to join us."

Randall stared at Erin, his eyes hard. Focused. Alert. He had noticed how she wasn't questioning why Daermarn didn't trust Randall, and she didn't seem worried about it either, which probably made him worried. I knew he wanted her under his thumb. Both of us for that matter.

"Daermarn made a request," I continued. "He asked for immunity for himself and the rest of the settlement. Otherwise, his people will withdraw from the unit."

Randall grunted under his breath. "Fine. I'll grant them immunity. But I'm not done with them. We'll schedule another day when you two will go back and convince the other half to join us."

I bowed my head slightly. "Yes, sir." I took a step back, ready to turn and leave.

"I have another job for you two," Randall said, looking from me to Erin and back to me. "I want you to find Zachary—and dispose of him."

Erin inhaled a sharp breath.

I frowned. "Dispose of him?"

"Yes," Randall said, annoyed. "He's becoming a threat and risks exposing the unit before we're ready to reveal it to our society."

"But—"

"You two have magical deals with me," Randall continued, cutting Erin's protest before it even started. "Contracts, you might want to call them. If I tell you to do something, you do it. And right now, I'm telling you that Zachary is a liability. He needs to be found and disposed of. Understood?"

"Yes, sir," I spoke first.

"You can go now." Randall lowered his gaze to the papers on his desk.

I turned to walk to the door, but Erin remained in her spot, glaring at Randall with her hands closed into tight fists. I grabbed her wrist and dragged her out of the office, before she did or said something she would regret.

She resisted at first, but then she let me drag her into the cold night. Once the chilly wind hit our faces, she woke up. With a knot between her brows, she tugged her arm free from my grip.

"You weren't serious, right?" she asked. "We aren't going to kill Zachary, right?"

"Erin ..."

She took a large step back, her frown deepening. "He didn't really do anything wrong. We're the ones who messed up his life."

"I know that, but it's an order from Randall," I explained. "We can't resist it, not for long. And if we try to resist it, he'll manipulate us even more. I bet that if you move against his wishes, he'll expose your true heritage before you're ready." I knew Randall had talked to her about it, and they planned on telling everyone that she was a half-demon when he introduced the Black Knight Unit. "He'll also punish, or even kill me for disobeying him. After all, he owns me now."

Her lower lip trembled into a small pout. "This isn't fair."

I scoffed. "My life hasn't been fair. Not even once."

"Don't say things like that."

"Why not?"

She fixed those intense golden eyes on mine. "Because then I feel like hugging and comforting you."

Holy fuck.

Trying hard not imagining how amazing it would be to have her hold me and comfort me, I cleared my throat. "Anyway, there's no way around it. We'll have to kill Zachary."

19

ERIN

LIKE REY HAD SAID, I COULD FEEL THE HEADMASTER'S ORDERS deep in my bones, demanding to be answered. Because of it, I looked for Zachary, but not very hard. Since we got the orders to kill him two weeks ago, Zachary hadn't been seen on campus and his wife didn't know where he was. So while Rey ran around, trying to find him, I focused on the preparations for the Spring Hunters' Ball, which was coming up soon.

One morning, I was supposed to meet Thierry to check if all the guests had gotten their invitations and start the RSVP list, but he didn't come. Instead, he sent me a note saying he could do that by himself, and I should help with the decorations.

Feeling like I had been dumped, I went to the ballroom on the first floor of the Aster building—it was an impressive oval room, large and tall, with long dark framed windows, smooth beige stone flooring, and black vines and thorns chandeliers. The academy crest, probably taller than me, hung from one of the walls. The room was opulent and oozed importance; I could imagine the place filled with tables and chairs, and people dressed in fancy gowns and suits.

In the middle of the room, Ava sat at a big round table, going over a list of the materials spread out around her.

She glanced over the clipboard in her arms and instantly frowned. "What are you doing here?"

"I was sent to help with decorations," I told her, though all I wanted was to pretend I hadn't heard that and walk away.

"There isn't much to do now," she said, her voice tight. "I won't start decorations for another week or so."

I could see why, since the ball was still two weeks away. "Is there any other way I can help?" If I had a choice, I wouldn't spend one more minute around her, but I really didn't want to be called out later for being assigned the tasks and not delivering them.

"No, there's nothing." She glanced down to her list. "The fabric and other supplies I'll need arrived for the decorations, so now I'm making sure the order is all here." She put the clipboard down and started rummaging through the boxes on the tables, looking for something. The large table was so crammed, one of the boxes slid to the floor.

I picked it up. "For the record, I don't like you either, but I think you could use a hand. Tell me the item name and number, or whatever, and I'll find it."

She stared at me for a moment. "All right. I'll let you help me, but no talking!"

I shrugged. "Just the way I want it."

She grunted before rattling out the number and model of some paper, and I dug into the boxes, searching for it.

To my surprise, Ava was able to keep quiet while we worked. And we kind of worked well together. She told me which box I would find the item, the item number, and I separated it into another pile, and she checked the item off her list.

I frowned, just now realizing she was working alone. "Where's Doreen?"

"Busy," she said before telling me about another roll of fabric.

I found it a second later and fished it out of the box. "So odd. Thierry didn't give me an explanation, but since he's not here, I bet he's busy too." I placed the fabric roll on the pile of checked items. "Do the hunters have something going on?" Suddenly, Ava lowered her head and her shoulders shook. I froze. "Are you crying?"

Ava shook her head, but it was obvious she was crying. I stared at her for another moment, not sure what to do. Then, I fished some tissue from my tote bag and offered it to her.

I might not like her, but I couldn't ignore such earnest crying either.

She took the tissue paper from me. "Thanks," she muttered before blowing her nose.

I sat down beside her. "What's wrong?"

"It's Harvey," she said in a low voice. I rolled my eyes. Really? She wanted to talk to me about Harvey now? But her next words shocked me to the core. "He's missing."

I held my breath. "What?"

She lifted her blue eyes to me. "I went to his dorm room last night to talk to him, but when I got there, his door was half-open and there was blood on the floor. I called the guards. I was sent away, but Doreen told me to be quiet about it." Her lips trembled. "She said that they don't want to start a panic. School is supposed to be safe, and if students start vanishing like that, parents will start yanking kids out of the academy."

"That doesn't make sense," I muttered, thinking.

"Right? I understand Doreen's reservations, but there's something odd going on. When Brianne fell from the tower last semester, we all knew about it a few minutes later. This time, it has been over twelve hours and no one knows about it yet."

I frowned. It did sound odd. "When was the last time you saw him?"

She sniffed, trying to stop crying. "Yesterday morning, during class."

I thought about my schedule. I didn't have any afternoon classes with him yesterday. Could he have disappeared then?

"I'm having trouble just sitting here and working on this while our friend is missing," I said.

"That's why this shit is taking so long. Because I can't focus." She dropped the clipboard on the table. "What do you suggest we do?"

"I say we go investigate this ourselves."

One corner of her lips tugged up. "I like that idea."

* * *

Now that I knew about Harvey's disappearance, I felt an urge to do something, and yet, the academy went on as if nothing had happened. While Ava and I walked to the Snapdragon building, the other students walked to and from the Statice and Orchid buildings, coming and going to classes. Professors, most who probably knew what was going on, ushered everyone inside as if they would get bad marks for being late.

But I had seen a few more guards than usual patrolling the pathways between the buildings.

When we got to the third floor of the Snapdragon building, the building's right side, where Harvey's room was located, was closed off. A guard stood in the hallway, telling people that there was a problem in one of the bathrooms and they were working on it.

Right.

"What do we do now?" Ava asked in a low voice.

"We need a distraction," I said, looking around.

"I can come up with something." She headed for the stairs. Like a C-rated movie actress, Ava pretended to trip right on the first step. She yelled and half-climbed and half-rolled down the rest of the stairs.

I watched in shock as she really went for it. She might not be that much of a bad actress after all.

Then, the guard took a step forward, watching us.

This was my chance. "Holy shit, my friend is hurt. Please help."

The guard hesitated, but finally he walked to me, then rushed down the stairs to help Ava.

Without wasting a second, I ran down the hallway and into Harvey's room.

I gasped, a hand over my mouth.

There was blood on the floor and in his bed. Some of his books were overturned, and some pens and markers were scattered around the place.

Harvey hadn't simply disappeared. He had been taken.

I inhaled deeply and summoned my magic—like I had

learned from one of the books Claire found for me. I opened my senses and let the air around the room talk to me.

I felt it then. Demonic magic sparkled in several places in response to mine.

Whoever took Harvey was either a demon or had some sort of demonic power.

20

I HAD SPENT THE ENTIRE FUCKING NIGHT INVESTIGATING WITH the guards and the handful of Blackthorn Hunters who had been on campus.

And despite knowing it had been a demon who took Harvey, I didn't find any more clues.

Tired to the bone and starving, I headed to the cafeteria late in the morning, when I knew the lunch crowd hadn't arrived yet, snatched some food from the kitchen while it was being cooked, and sat at a corner table to eat.

My plan was to refuel, doze off for a few minutes in my bed, then resume investigating.

I was halfway done with my plate when Erin and Ava entered the cafeteria and headed straight to me.

I frowned, instantly suspicious. What the fuck were the two of them doing together?

They sat down, Erin to my right and Ava to my left.

"What's going on?" I asked.

"We know Harvey is missing," Ava said.

And just like that, I lost my appetite. "I told Randall you

would be the first to notice that, and this secrecy wouldn't last long." I pushed my plate away. "What do you know?"

"We know it was a demon who took him," Erin said. "I could feel demonic magic in his room."

This was getting worse. "How did you get into his room? A guard was posted there."

Erin and Ava shared a glance.

"I improvised," Ava said, pointing to the bruise on her hand. "Anyway, we know you're investigating his disappearance and we want to know more about it."

"We want to help," Erin said. Her golden eyes softened. "Please."

How could I resist when she looked at me like that? I let out a long sigh. "I also detected demonic magic in his room, but I'm not sure if it was from a pure demon or a half-demon. My guess is that whoever took him, teletransported out of the academy but—"

"Right," Erin muttered. "Some higher demons can teletransport."

"—I can't track him. I've tried, but the spell I know doesn't work. It's like whoever took him put a hex on Harvey that prevents him from being tracked."

"If we can't track him, how will we find him?" Ava asked, obviously shaken by all of this.

"We'll find a way," Erin said, her words sounding true, as if she really believed in it. Or as if she too had to believe in it. "We need to ask Claire. She's read all the books at the academy, and more. She might know of different tracking spells, more powerful ones that will work despite a hex."

Ava nodded once and shot up. Erin was next.

I shook my head. "If anyone finds out I'm letting you help me—"

"We'll tell them we forced you," Erin said quickly.

"Why don't we worry about this later?" Ava asked. "Our priority is finding Harvey. After that, I'll be okay with any punishment."

She was right. Who cared about rules and punishments when there was a life on the line? First, we find Harvey. Later we could worry about all the other fucked up things.

I stood with them. "Let's go."

"Any idea where Claire is?" Ava asked as we walked out of the cafeteria.

"Her class must have just finished," Erin said. "At the Orchid building. Usually, we meet up between buildings and come to the cafeteria for lunch together."

"Lead the way," I told her.

Hugging her jacket tighter, Erin walked around the Statice building. There was a cold breeze blowing every few minutes, but other than that, the weather was finally starting to look better and less chilly. But I knew I shouldn't get my hopes too high yet. After all, here in Colorado, it could snow well into May.

We walked past the courtyard and toward the main door of the Orchid building. Then Erin skidded to a stop, her eyes round.

Ava and I halted with her and followed her line of sight.

A few yards from us, Tanner jabbed his finger at Claire's face. "Are you fucking serious?" he yelled. The students walking by paused to stare, but no one did anything. "You're so fucking stupid!"

Beside me, Erin balled her hands into fists. "That little douche." With a murderous glint in her eyes, Erin took a step forward. I clasped my hand around her wrist and held her back. "Let me kick his ass!"

Tanner continued yelling, "I don't know what I saw in you. You're ridiculous!"

Claire cowered before him, her eyes full of tears.

"No, leave him to me." I dropped Erin's hand and turned to the fucking douche, who would get his ass handed to him in a flat three seconds.

But before I could do anything, Harper ran into the picture, and with a battle cry, landed a beautiful flying side kick to Tanner's ribs. The douche fell on the hard stone pavement with a cry. Cursing Harper and her mother, he shot up, ready to retaliate, but Harper was ready for him.

"Not today," she snarled before she did a back wheel kick that hit him squared in the chest, then a series of punches on his stomach.

Students formed a circle around the three of them. Erin pushed through the crowd, trying to get to her friend, and I went for Harper and Tanner. As much as I liked the fact that he was getting what he deserved, I knew if this persisted, Harper would be in trouble for it.

Dodging their attacks, I was able to wedge myself between them. "Stop it!" Harper let go instantly, but Tanner lunged at her. I put my arm out and stopped him though. "I can immobilize you," I said in a low voice. "But I think you don't want me to do that because it'll be embarrassing for you."

He glared at me, visibly agitated.

A couple of feet to the side, Erin hugged Claire. Ava stood quietly by them.

I had been able to stop the fight, but not soon enough.

Professor Crimson marched past the crowd. "All of you! Go back to your schedule right this instant!" Mutters rose among the students as they slowly dispersed out and left the scene. Then he turned his deadly stare to Tanner and Harper. "You two are in big trouble. Come with me." Next, he looked at his daughter. "Claire Breevort! You're in even bigger trouble."

"But—"

Crimson cut Erin a nasty stare, shutting her up. "Unless you want to share in their punishment, I suggest you stay out of this."

Erin seemed like she wasn't done with it, but Claire held her hands. "It's okay. Stay here. I'll be right back."

Wiping her tears, Claire followed her father away, along with Harper and Tanner.

"That was crazy," Ava muttered.

"It's unfair to Claire," Erin said, upset. "She did nothing wrong."

"I know," Ava gasped. "What about Harper? She really beat Tanner up!"

"It was wrong," I said. "I was going to do the same, but it was still wrong." Erin looked at me, her eyes suddenly soft. What had I done? I averted my gaze before I said something stupid. "Anyway, Claire is gone now."

"Shit," Erin muttered, staring in the distance, to her friend who was entering the Aster building with her father. "Do we have any other leads or clues so we can do something while we wait for Claire's punishment to end?"

Ava scoffed. "Her punishment hasn't even started. I doubt it's going to end anytime soon." She lifted the sleeve of her jacket and checked her wristwatch. "And I have class soon. Not that I'm in the mood for class, but I failed an assignment this last week and I need to make up for it."

"We can wait," I said. "Go to class. If Claire isn't back by the time it's over, we'll come up with something else."

"All right. Later," she said, before walking away.

I turned to Erin. "What about you?"

She took a few steps to a wooden bench lining the court-yard and sat down. "No classes until later."

I sat down beside her. "So we just wait?"

She shrugged. "What else can we do right now?"

"Nothing," I muttered.

Erin twisted to the side and leaned back on the bench, resting her arms on the back, and lying her head on her arms. "I'll just close my eyes for a bit, then."

I frowned at her. "Didn't sleep well?"

Eyes already closed, she shook her head. "Haven't slept well in months."

I wanted to ask her more about it, but I stopped myself. When was I going to learn that I couldn't keep asking her those kinds of questions? I couldn't hide my interest in her when I did.

I kept quiet and, in a few minutes, Erin's breathing slowed and her muscles relaxed. She really fell asleep, right here on this cold bench with the occasional chilly wind. At least the sun was high and a little warm today.

An urge to bring a blanket to cover her and to pull her closer to me so she could be more comfortable lying on my shoulder hit me hard. I had to curl my hands and stare out, trying to think of anything else but the beautiful girl beside me.

The girl with the sweet rose scent that filled my nostrils every time she was nearby. The girl with a perfect nose and the faint freckles over it. The girl with the long lashes, the delicate brows, the pink, plump lips. The girl with the luscious black hair that now fell down her shoulders and back like a curtain. The girl who I wanted to touch and kiss and take care of more than anything else in the world.

I reached up and hovered my fingertips over the features of her beautiful face, trying to commit them to my memory. The end goal was to let go of her completely. To walk away and not look back. I knew that was still far away because until I was sure she was a hundred percent safe from the Supreme Demon, I wasn't going anywhere, but before I left for good, I wanted to stare at her for many, many hours, so I would never forget how breathtakingly beautiful she was.

Although, it wasn't just her beauty that took my breath away, or how hot she was with her lean body and right curves. It was everything about her. She was kind and caring. She was a good friend and a good student. She worked harder than anyone I knew to catch up with everything at the academy and be able to stay here. She tried to keep herself upbeat even though she knew her fate was gruesome.

And she never gave up.

Sometimes, I wished she wouldn't give up on me—even though I pushed her away so fucking often. At some point, her insistence that there was something between us would wear me out and I would give in.

That was one fucking idea.

No, no. I was working so hard to not put her in more danger; I wasn't going to mess it all up now.

I scooted a foot to the side, putting more distance between us, and looked at the Blackthorn tree. It still amazed me that the tree had given an original Dawnblade to Erin. It had to be a hidden meaning to that, but what?

Suddenly, Erin jerked in her sleep. Concerned, I turned back to her. A second later, she frowned and a tremor ran through her body.

"No," she whispered. She trembled again.

I clasped her shoulders. "Erin, wake up."

She jerked against my hold and said louder, "Please, no!"

I cupped her face. "Erin, wake up!" Her eyes snapped open and she pulled back, almost falling off the bench if I hadn't held on to her arms. "Hey, it's me." Her breathing came out in little gasps and her eyes darted side to side. "Erin, look at me." Her eyes found mine. I leaned closer. "You're fine. Everything is okay now."

Her shoulders relaxed and her breathing slowed down. She slumped forward and I caught her in my arms. Forgetting about all the logic, I pulled her to me and held her tight.

"I'm sorry," she whispered, her face tucked into my neck.

Holy fuck, how I wanted to be like this forever. "For?"

She pulled back, making me agonize on the inside, and shrugged. "For freaking out on you."

"That's nothing," I told her. She was still seated right beside me, her hips pressed to my legs, her shoulder just a few inches from my chest. "Though I'm worried now. What was that?"

She stared at the tree in the middle of the courtyard. "I've been having nightmares since that night."

"That night?"

"Yeah, that one. When Asmodeus told me who my father was, and Randall killed him."

I frowned. Not because she had mentioned my father, but because I was curious about these nightmares. "What are they about?"

"Brianne and Cindy," she whispered. "They come to me, looking mostly like zombies, and they ask for help. I try going to them, I try helping them, but I never can. Demons come and kill them right before my eyes, while they scream for me, and then the demons come for me. I know they are night-mares, but they are so real and terrifying. I can never go back to sleep after that." That was why she wasn't sleeping well, then. Her golden eyes filled with tears. "I just want them to stop."

Before I could stop myself, I wrapped my arm over her shoulder and tugged her to me again. "It's okay, now." Her head rested on my shoulder. "I'm here and I won't let anything happen to you." My hand on hers, I ran my thumb over her wrist, where the mark still marred her skin. "After we find Harvey, I'll help you find out how to stop the night-mares." Erin stilled against me. "What's wrong?"

Slowly, she rose her head and locked her eyes on mine. "Nothing," she said, her voice low. My eyes flickered to her lips. It would be easy to kiss her right now. All I had to do was erase the inch between us. Just like that. "There's nothing wrong when you comfort me like this. In fact, everything feels right. There's a connection between us, Rey. I know it and you know it."

I gulped. I couldn't deny it. The connection between us was bigger than life, but I also couldn't tell her that. Reluc-tantly, I leaned back and shook my head. "I don't know what you're talking about."

"I'll tell you, then." Her brows slammed down. "A twin soul bond mark appeared above my chest a few months ago. Supposedly, the guy I shared the soul bond with has the same mark. And I think that guy is you."

"You're mistaken," I said, trying to keep my tone deadpan. "I don't have any marks on my body."

She narrowed her knowing eyes at me. "Can you prove it?"

I channeled my magic, a tiny sliver so she wouldn't be

able to detect it, and covered the mark up. "Above your chest, you said, right?" Erin nodded and I started unbuttoning my shirt. I pulled it open and showed her my bare torso with no marks in sight. "See?"

"It can't be." Erin's eyes rounded, as if she was in shock. "If it's not you, then who is it?"

This was too fucking much for me. I stood up, in need of space from her. Hadn't I just hugged her? "I don't know."

"How am I supposed to love someone else if I can't seem to let you go?" she mused, her voice low.

Love.

She had said love.

Did she love me?

The thought made my heart skip a beat. Fuck, this was all so messed up. "I'm certainly not the one you're looking for."

Her shoulders sagged, as if she gave up.

I didn't say anything for a moment, but I really thought about telling her another lie so I could wait for Ava and Claire somewhere else. Somewhere away from her.

Erin shot to her feet, her eyes on her wristwatch. "Ava should have been back by now." She glanced at the Aster building. "And what about Claire?"

Glad for the change in subject, I said, "Claire is probably in detention of sorts now. Why don't we go after Ava first?"

Without looking at me, Erin nodded. In silence, we crossed the courtyard right in the center, walked around the Blackthorn tree, and halted at the Statice building entrance, when Ava's friends, Stella and Ruby, walked out.

"Have you guys seen Ava?" Erin asked them.

Stella wrinkled her nose at Erin, and Ruby flipped her hair as if she didn't matter.

Irritation snaked through my chest. "Answer her. Where's Ava?"

The two of them looked at me, wary, but not disgusted.

"She's in the restroom," Stella said.

"How long ago was that?"

Ruby looked down at her watch. "About ten minutes ago."

Erin frowned. "Didn't you go after her?"

Stella shrugged one of her shoulders. "She never goes after us, why would we go after her? We've waited for her this long. When she's ready, she'll find us in our next class."

Wow, Ava called these girls friends. Perhaps they really deserved each other.

"If you want to talk to her, why don't you go find her?" Ruby asked, her tone clearly annoyed.

"I'll do that," Erin said, walking past the two girls and into the building.

She took the first left and ran down the hallway. I ran after her. When she pushed into the female restroom, I paused at the door, suddenly overcome by manners, but when I saw the scene before us, I barged in.

"What the fuck?" I asked, glancing around.

Blood stained the floor and one of the sinks, and Ava's books and purse were scattered on the floor.

"She was taken too," Erin said, her face pale.

To make sure we were dealing with the same demon, I channeled my magic and sensed the power in the restroom. The magic sparkled in response to mine—the same one from Harvey's room.

"It's the same demon," I said.

Erin turned to me, her eyes downcast. "Now Ava is missing too."

21

ERIN

This couldn't be happening. First Harvey, now Ava. We had to put a stop to this.

"Don't you have to report this?" I asked Rey, knowing that the headmaster's grip on him was much tighter than on me.

"I have to, but that doesn't mean I will." He glanced at me, those gray eyes almost silver. "Come on. We need Claire." He exited the restroom and I followed, glad to leave such a gruesome scene. After I walked out, Rey closed the door and infused his magic on it. "Now no one will be able to enter and see it, at least not for a couple of hours."

Then we walked out of the building.

I stayed a few steps behind him on purpose as we walked to the Aster building. After what had just happened between us, I needed space.

Holy shit, I had practically confessed my feelings to him. I had told him about the soul bond and that I hoped he was the one for me.

But he wasn't. He had even shown me his chest, and there was no mark there. At that moment, my heart shattered into a million tiny pieces. Rey wasn't my soulmate. Then how could anyone else be?

My embarrassment demanded I either run or put a sack over my head so I could hide, but unfortunately, two of my friends were missing. My love life drama could wait a little longer.

Rey and I entered the Aster building, determined to find Claire and break her out of any punishments, but we were surprised to see her seated on the stairs in the lobby.

With Tanner by her side.

Anger rippled through me and I stomped to them.

"Come with me, Claire." I extended my hand to her. "You don't need to endure this jerk anymore."

Claire glanced from me to Tanner. Tanner nodded at her. She returned her gaze to me. "It's fine, Erin. We're fine now."

I narrowed my eyes. "What do you mean you're fine now?"

"We're—"

Tanner wrapped a hand around her waist. "We made up." He waved us off with his other arm. "You can leave now."

The anger inside me only sparked more. "We aren't leaving without Claire. Please, Claire, come with us. We need you."

"It's important," Rey said, his tone serious.

Holding her hand, Tanner stood. "She can't. She's coming with me."

"What the hell?" I gritted my teeth. "Claire?"

She looked at me with puppy eyes but ended up shaking her head. "Sorry, Erin, I can't." She stood beside Tanner. "I'll see you later, okay."

Tanner started walking past us, jerking her with more force than necessary. "Bye," he said in a sing-song tone.

"Claire," I called after her. "Please, we need you!" She didn't even glance back as she left the building, her hand firmly in Tanner's. "I can't believe this. Why is she going with that jerk?"

"I don't get it either, but we don't have time for that right now," Rey said. "We need to figure out how to find Harvey and Ava on our own."

Shit, he was right. We couldn't wait for Claire anymore. She would hear from me later, but there were more pressing matters in need of attention. "Right. Any ideas how we're going to do that?"

Rey shook his head. "All I can think of is going back to the restroom or Harvey's room and searching for more clues."

"We already did that."

"I know, but it's all I have."

Not liking this feeling that there was so much to do but no direction to follow, I nodded. "Okay. Let's go back to the restroom. It's closer."

Rey and I walked back to the Statice building. I felt like I was waltzing in a zigzag pattern around campus all day. And right now, I should be heading to class. Shit, I would get an absence and a negative mark for the day.

I shook my head. *Focus, Erin.* Harvey and Ava were more important than classes and grades.

Once inside the Statice building, Rey and I headed to the female restroom. The door was still untouched, with Rey's magic strong. After undoing his spell, Rey pushed the door open and we stepped inside.

I wrinkled my nose at the scene. I had already seen the blood, the mess, but I doubted it wouldn't bother me each time I looked at it.

Inhaling deeply, Rey closed his eyes and called his power.

A moment later, I felt it like a fingertip running up my arms, a tangible thing that sent a chill down my spine. His magic filled the room, making the demonic power crack and stir to life.

"If only I could get a better hold on it," he muttered. With eyes still open, he reached for me and grasped my hands. "Open your magic to me."

I frowned at our joined hands. We had done this before, used our combined powers to close the demonic portal. It could work once again. I took in a long breath and channeled my magic. Once I felt it tickling inside me, I sent it to him. He easily took hold of my magic and added it to his. Our combined power overflowed the restroom, making it nearly suffocating.

The demonic magic reacted, kindling even faster and more violently, as if it was alive. As if it was a tiny demon screaming and fighting us.

But then I felt it. This magic wasn't a hundred percent demonic. It was like Rey's and mine.

I gasped. "It was a half-demon."

Rey snapped his eyes open. "That's what I got from it too."

I dropped my magic and pulled my hands from his. As much as I liked him holding me, he had made it clear he didn't want me. He had even proved he wasn't the one destined for me.

"But who?"

"Zachary," Rey said. "He had that breakdown. He must be acting on his promise to make us pay."

But it didn't make sense. If Zachary wanted me to pay, he would have taken Claire, not Harvey or Ava. Well, not that I would ever stand for them getting hurt because of me, but

Harvey wasn't as close to me as Claire. And Ava ... I barely put up with her, much less being friends.

Either way, I couldn't think of any other half-demon we knew who could have snuck into the academy and taken Harvey and Ava.

"We need to find Zachary, right now," I said. "Any ideas where he could be?"

Rey shook his head. "No, but I think I know where we can start."

* * *

REY AND I HEADED TO ZACHARY'S HOUSE AT THE EDGE OF Chasseur Ville. On the way, we were tensely quiet, but my mind was full.

Besides my worry for Harvey and Ava, I also thought of poor Claire, who I would have to sit down and have a nice talk with. She not only pushed me away, but she was dating a douchebag who had no respect for her. That was unacceptable.

But more than that, my thoughts revolved around the man seated behind the steering wheel a few inches from me.

I stole a glance at him. The sun was setting, bathing him with golden light, and giving him a godlike air. Holy shit, he was so freaking handsome. I liked every detail about him. His sharp nose, his set eyebrows, his gray, sometimes silver eyes, his red lips, the rough edges of his chin and his jaw. Until him, I hadn't thought blond guys were for me, but the dirty blond hair worked for Rey. In fact, he made everything work for him. The student uniform, a suit and dress pants, even a long winter coat—it all went well with his tall, ripped body.

Being so handsome, and always there when I needed him, why couldn't he be the one from the soul bond? It was a sick joke from fate. Make me fall in love with one guy and then bind me to another.

I gasped out loud.

Holy shit, I loved him.

I loved Rey.

I hadn't really thought of the word love for us. I had just thought he might be my soulmate. That I liked him enough for that.

But now I knew it with certain clarity: I loved Rey.

Tears of frustration came to my eyes.

"What is it?" Rey asked, glancing at me. "What happened?"

"Nothing." I waited until he looked at the road again to wipe the tears from my eyes before they fell. I felt stupid for wanting to cry because of this, but this agony inside me was so strong, it was hard not to. "It's nothing."

I could see he didn't buy it, which didn't help. How did he want me to let him go, when he looked at me like that—like he cared, like he could slay the entire underworld to make sure I was all right?

I had to be imagining things. Because if that was right, he would have told me he liked me too—that he loved me too. He wouldn't push me away.

Right?

Honestly, I didn't know anything anymore.

Rey parked his car in front of Zachary's house. He looked at me. "Zachary is probably unstable right now. Just ... be careful."

My heart yanked. Why did he do this to me?

Without a word, I climbed out the car and headed to the

house at the end of the driveway. Rey was right behind me. I rang the doorbell and waited.

I wasn't sure what I was expecting, but when his wife—or ex-wife, rather—opened the door, I was surprised. From what Rey had told me, Zachary said Susan had left, which made me think he was still living here, and she wasn't.

"Hi, hm, I'm not sure you remember me—"

"I do," Susan said, cutting me off. Her tone was guarded, just like the glint in her eyes. "You're Erin, and you're Rey. You're probably here to see Zachary."

"Yes," Rey said.

She crossed her arms. "You won't find him here. I kicked him out a couple of weeks ago."

"Do you know where we can find him?" I asked.

"Why?" Her tone was more guarded by the second.

Rey and I exchanged a glance. Maybe it was wrong of me to tell her the truth, but at the same time, she deserved it.

"The thing is, Zachary isn't in a good place right now." I told her about his meltdown, his threats, and about how Harvey and Ava were missing, and we thought he had been the one to take them away. "I know this sounds crazy."

"No, it doesn't." Her chest deflated and her eyes filled with tears. "It's all my fault. If I had talked to him, if he had explained better, if I had been more open, none of this would have happened."

"Are you saying you know he took our friends?" Rey asked.

"I don't know that. But going crazy, doing big things he regrets later, that sounds like Zachary." She shook her head. "This half-demon thing scared the hell out of me."

"You know, being a half-demon isn't a bad thing," Rey

said, his voice soft. "We're half-demons and we're definitely not evil."

She stared at us, clearly not convinced but not disgusted or afraid either. "If only he would come back and talk to me."

"Listen, we're afraid he's hurting our friends," I said. "Do you have any idea where he might be?"

She hesitated. "There's a cottage outside Chasseur Ville, following the north dirt road. It was his grandmother's, and he used to visit it a lot when he needed to think." She shrugged. "But I'm not sure."

"That's enough for now," Rey said before turning to me. "We should check it out."

I nodded once. Then I looked at Susan again. "Thank you for helping. If Zachary comes back, try to keep him here. If we don't find anyone at the cottage, we'll come back to check with you."

"No, wait, I'm coming with you," she said, already stepping out the door.

Rey shot me a worried look.

"Look, we don't know how Zachary will be," I said. "It might be best if you stay behind."

She puffed her chest. "I'm the only one who knows exactly where this cottage is. Unless you want to spend hours searching for it, then go ahead."

Holy shit. When she put it that way ...

22

REY

IT WAS HARD TO CONVINCE SUSAN TO STAY IN THE CAR WHILE we checked the cottage first, but after some reasoning, she relented.

Erin and I approached the cabin with careful steps, as if booby traps would jump out at us at any moment. We spied inside a window and found our theory to be true: Zachary was in the cabin with both Harvey and Ava. Tied to chairs in the middle of the living room and their mouths bound, they looked like they had seen better days.

Beside me, Erin tensed. "We've got to do something." She channeled her magic.

"We will, but let's not rush into things," I said. "If we surprise him, he might react even worse."

She groaned. "Fine. What do you suggest?"

I wasn't too sure. What I didn't want was to surprise him and have him hurt Harvey and Ava. We had to either immobilize him or approach him carefully and try to reason with him.

"I think—"

"I know you're out there," Zachary said from inside the cottage. "Stop hiding like cowards."

"Fuck," I muttered.

Erin went to the front door and opened it. Zachary stood in front of Harvey and Ava, his Dawnblade leveled at us. "I knew you would come for them," he said, satisfied.

Erin raised her hands before stepping into the cottage. "How did you know?"

I went inside with her, keeping her close.

"Because you've been flirting with Harvey," Zachary said, with a triumphant tone to his voice. "You like him. I saw you two on a date."

So that was why he took Harvey. Because he thought Erin and Harvey were together. The fucked up jerk wasn't paying attention. By now, even I knew Erin and Harvey's date hadn't worked out.

Right?

"What about Ava?" Erin asked.

"She was snooping around too much since the moment I took Harvey," he said. "You know how that saying goes. Wrong place, wrong time."

"Zachary, your problem is with us," I told him, my voice even. "Let them go and fix this with us."

"Fix this?" Zachary scoffed. "The only way to fix all this is if I could take my half-demon part and extinguish it. But since I can't do that, I'll have to accept who I am and kill you."

He threw a darkfire bolt at Erin. I pushed her aside, creating a hole between us; the bolt flew past. Another bolt zipped toward me, but I raised a shield in front of myself.

On the other side of the door, Erin called her Dawnblade. It was a sight to behold. That crude but powerful blade in her hand.

"No killing, right?" she asked, her eyes on the target.

I hesitated. Randall had asked us to kill him, and here he was, hurting our friends, attacking us ... wasn't he bad enough to kill now?

No. That was the old me, the demon under Asmodeus's thumb talking. I wasn't like that anymore. I would like to think that I had been like that because of the circumstances, not because it was me.

"Right," I said. We would find a way to stop him. If we needed to put him in one of the demon hunters' prisons, then we would do it.

But no killing.

Zachary let out a loud, crazed laugh. "You two are ridiculous."

Then he teletransported. He disappeared and appeared again right in front of Erin, startling her. He closed his hand around her throat and pushed her against the wall. "You're dead."

He pulled his sword back, ready to stab her.

Panic filled my senses. I summoned my Dawnblade and aimed it for his heart.

"Zachary, stop."

The clank of his sword hitting the floor rang through the room. Staring at his wife with wide eyes, he let go of Erin and stepped back. "Susan. What are you doing here?"

"I came to stop you," she said, her voice shaky. "I came to tell you that I overreacted. That I should have listened to you, talked to you. That I should have understood." She glanced at Erin, then at Harvey and Ava, who were jerking against the ropes around them, as if they would fade away. "But it seems I was wrong about you."

"No, no, no." Zachary took two steps toward her. Susan

kept the distance by stepping back. "Susan, please." He held her hand and pulled her inside the cottage, between all of us.

I went to Erin, who had one of her hands around her neck. "Are you okay?"

She nodded, breathing deeply. "I will be."

"Zachary, what have you done?" Susan asked, with tears in her eyes.

"This is nothing, baby," Zachary said. "If you forgive me, I'll fix this. I'll let them go. I'll even apologize."

"Apologize?" Susan shook her head, the tears rolling down her face. "I don't think apologies can undo the damage you caused. Zach, what's happening to you?"

"It was all their fault!" He pointed to us. "If they hadn't found me, if he hadn't blackmailed me, if I hadn't joined the Black Knight unit. It's all their fault, baby."

"I'm afraid ..." She sniffed, trying to contain her tears. "I'm afraid I don't know you anymore." She took a step away from him. "I'm afraid I never really knew you."

"No, no, no." Immense desperation was clear in Zachary's eyes and voice. "Please, baby."

He reached for her, but she retreated more.

"Zachary," Erin called. "Come with us. We'll take you to the academy and—"

"No!" he roared, throwing a bolt of darkfire at Erin. "I'll never go back there!"

I jumped to Erin's side and deflected the bolt, twisting it in my hands, and releasing it back toward Zachary.

"Zack!" Arms open, Susan stepped in front of her husband.

The bolt hit her square in the chest. A bolt that was intended to hurt a half-demon, but that certainly was too strong for a human.

Susan whimpered. She glanced at Zachary, then crumbled to the floor.

I stared in horror.

I had killed her.

I had killed an innocent human.

The howl that came from Zachary's throat only increased the sudden pain and terror filling me. He summoned his Dawnblade and brought it to his chest, piercing it through his heart.

"No!" I cried.

Beside me, Erin gasped. A few steps back from the scene, Harvey and Ava watched everything, still.

And I stared at the two bodies on the floor. One charred in the chest, the other with bright red blood pooling underneath.

"I did that," I whispered. "It's my fault."

Erin turned to me. "What are you talking about?"

"I killed his wife, and he killed himself because of it." I stared into her golden eyes, looking for salvation in them.

But I didn't deserve any fucking salvation.

"That's ridiculous." She clasped her hands around my upper arms. "Rey, it's not your fault."

I wanted to believe her, I really did, but with my history, with my temper, with my blood, I knew it wasn't true. I had turned that bolt around and thrown it at Zachary.

If I hadn't done that, his wife wouldn't have died.

Muffles and mutters and stomps reached my ears. Harvey and Ava tried to scream and jump on their chairs to catch our attention.

I stepped back from Erin and went to them, my steps stiff, my movements automatic. I started untying Harvey. After a heavy sigh, Erin followed my lead and worked on freeing Ava.

"Ow," Harvey muttered once he was free. Weak, he slumped to the side of the chair, but I caught him. "Thanks."

Ava was in better shape than he was and didn't accept Erin's help to stand.

"What happened?" Erin asked.

"Zachary came to me in my room," Harvey said, as we walked out of the cottage. "We fought a little, but he used his magic on me. But then he teletransported and knocked me out as soon as we arrived here."

Erin frowned at Harvey, then Ava. "There was a lot of blood in your room, and in the restroom."

"Zachary healed the worst of our wounds with a special healing potion," Ava said, her voice quieter than usual.

"Zachary wasn't really a bad person," Erin mused. "Perhaps he was just an unhinged half-demon."

Ava scoffed. "If he wasn't evil, he wouldn't have taken us."

"If he was really evil, he wouldn't have healed your wounds," Erin protested.

Ava shot her a glare. "You know what? I'm not gonna argue with you about this. I'm done with all this shit." She slipped into the backseat of my car, ending the conversation.

Erin went to the backseat with Ava, and I helped Harvey to the passenger seat.

The only thing we talked about when riding back to the academy was what we were going to tell Randall and the others. Since I would probably have to write a report on all of this, I wanted it to be as close to the truth as possible: A mad Zachary had kidnapped Harvey and Ava. When Erin and I went to check on his wife to make sure she was okay—the biggest lie of my future report—we found Zachary. He attacked us, and in the heat of the battle, I ended up killing his wife. And overwhelmed with grief, Zachary took his own life.

At least Randall would be happy that his order of disposing of Zachary had been fulfilled.

Once we were back, Erin and I helped Harvey and Ava to the infirmary. Cecile, the head physician, took them in without many questions. I promised her I would report on this right away, and would come back to check on them tomorrow morning.

Wanting to be alone, I walked out of the Daffodil building. Before I reported this, I needed to clear my head, with the chilly air filling my lungs, and calm my traitor heart.

"Rey."

Her voice was the last thing I wanted to hear right now.

I should have ignored her, pretended I hadn't heard her, but I was tired of being a fucking jerk all the time.

I turned to her as she approached me. "Hey."

Erin halted two feet from me. "How are you feeling?"

I frowned. Was that a trick question? I shrugged. "Fucking great."

Those golden eyes narrowed at me. "Why are you lying to me? I noticed you were upset before. What can I do to help you?"

"Stay away from me," I said, loud and clear.

She flinched. "But—"

"No, Erin, I mean it." My hurt, my disappointment, and my frustration, all rolled up into one messy ball that quickly became pure anger. "Don't you fucking get it? For centuries, all I did was hurt people. I tricked them, and I killed them. Now, even when I'm trying not to be that bad, I end up hurting them."

"It wasn't your fault," she whispered.

"The hell it wasn't! I could have stopped that bolt. I could have tried another approach. But I threw it at him, knowing it would have hurt him." An invisible hand squeezed my chest. "And now two people are dead because of me."

"No, Rey, don't say that." She reached for me. "You're a good person; I know you are."

I took a step back, not letting her touch me. She didn't get it. She would never get it. Unless I told her all the fucked up things I did, unless I showed them to her, she wouldn't understand how tainted my past was.

How tainted my life continued to be.

"Erin, for once and for all, just ... stay away from me." Leaving my heart in her hands, I turned and walked away.

23

ERIN

So many things happened the next few days, it was a whirlwind, and at the same time, time dragged.

After that night with Zachary, that case, which had been quiet to begin with, was wrapped up quickly. Nobody knew what happened. Harvey and Ava were discharged from the infirmary the next day, and advised to take it slow for a while. Thankfully, none of them had terrible injures and they would heal nicely.

As for Zachary, Randall released a statement saying that he and his wife had died in an accident at the cottage outside Chasseur Ville. The school grieved and mourned and participated in a small funeral for them.

Claire had been spending less and less time with me. Whenever I brought up Tanner, she shut me out, or walked away. Afraid of losing my friend, I stopped bothering her about him. I kind of hated myself for that, but I didn't see another way. Unless he was stupid with her again. Then, I wouldn't have it. Thankfully, Tanner hadn't made any more scenes.

Meanwhile, Rey was being quieter and more isolated than ever.

Although he had told me to stay away from him, and it freaking hurt, I wondered if a part of it was his hurt talking. Maybe he wanted me to stay away, but it didn't hate me. I was worried about him. But he wouldn't let me get close to ask how he was doing. So, I sent Harvey. Which didn't work, because he was avoiding Harvey too.

But there was only so much I could do besides worrying.

For two weeks, I tried keeping my mind on class stuff, tests and assignments, and helping organize the Spring Hunter Ball. Things were odd between Ava and me, but whenever Thierry was busy with demon hunter stuff, I helped her with decorations.

One afternoon before the day of the ball, though, Ava said she had other stuff to do, and I took over for her, finishing up decorating the ballroom, and Thierry helped me.

While we set up the tablecloths and the fancy flower arrangements in the center of the tables, Thierry seemed to come back to his old self—more or less. He would smile at me, as if he was flirting, but I noticed there was still some reservation there.

I didn't know what to make of it, though.

So, I didn't. I continued doing my job as if it was the only thing that mattered right now.

I picked up a big box with fabric napkins from the cart in the middle of the room, but then it was taken from me.

"Let me help you with that," Thierry said. He put the box on one of the tables and grinned at me. "There."

I frowned at him. "Thank you." But I could have done that, even if the box was a little heavy.

I picked up a handful of napkins from the box and started folding them the way I had been told to.

Thierry followed my lead and started folding fabric napkins too. "Erin, I want to talk to you about something."

"What is it?"

"I found out you helped the female fae escape from West Hill a few weeks ago," he said.

My hands froze. I looked up at him. So that was why he was acting strange and avoiding me. "How—?"

"It doesn't matter." He shook his head. "I found out, was pissed about it, and I told Randall, who said he was going to talk to you. I'm sorry if you got in trouble because of me."

I didn't know if that was amusing or concerning. Randall knew I had helped Farrah escape from the demon hunters, but he hadn't done anything to punish me. That was really weird.

"It's okay," I said, still wary of where this was going.

"I know you probably didn't do it on purpose," he continued. "You were probably just scared and feeling a little pity for the strange creature. I understand, I swear I do. But you have to keep one thing in mind: Supernaturals are evil. All of them. If she hadn't needed your help, that fae would have killed you without a thought."

I really doubted that. Farrah had been nothing more than a scared and friendly fae. If I could have gone back in time, I would have done the same, if not more. She deserved my help.

"If you say so," was my automatic response. I wouldn't argue with him about this, because I knew it wouldn't get anywhere.

"Erin, I have to ask, do you know where she went?"

I shook my head, glad I wasn't lying about that. "I don't." Though, if I knew, I wouldn't tell him.

"It's okay. I'll find her at some point." He continued folding napkins with me and spreading them around the table. Then he stopped suddenly. "One more thing. Although you lied, I still like you, and I was wondering if you want to be my date to the ball tomorrow night?"

I stared at him, surprised by the question. I mean, a couple of weeks ago, before he started avoiding me, I thought he would ask me, but then he changed.

And now the question came out of the blue.

I opened my mouth to tell him no, but pressed my lips tight before the word could come out. Why wasn't I going with him? Because he was an advocate that all supernaturals were evil? So were ninety-nine percent of the people inside this academy and I still liked a bunch of them. Because I was still hoping that Rey would ask me to go with him? That might be more accurate, but I also knew it would never happen. Waiting for Rey would only lead to more heartbreak.

Going to the ball with Thierry didn't mean that I liked him, and that I hoped he was my soulmate, right? It was only for fun, a good time between friends. That could happen, right? Besides, Claire was going with Tanner. I would have to go with Ava or alone.

Thierry was a much better choice.

I didn't think about it. I just went with it. "Sure. I would love to."

The grin that spread over his lips made me think he hoped for more. "Great."

* * *

BECAUSE OF THE BALL, THE STUDENTS HAD BEEN GIVEN permission to visit Chasseur Ville to go shopping.

Despite the tense mood between us, Claire had insisted we both go. But while walking down the streets of Chasseur Ville—unusually empty at this time of the day—Claire seemed to be nervous. Each sudden sound made her jump, and she kept looking over her shoulder as if a demon would lunge at her any second.

She veered toward the village's fanciest dress shop, where half of the girls in the school were currently trying on gowns.

I grabbed her wrist and said, "How about we go for ice cream first?"

She tilted her head. "Ice cream? In this cold?"

It wasn't too cold today, but it was still a far cry from a nice spring day.

"Ice cream is still ice cream, no matter the weather."

She pointed to the store. "If we don't go now, we'll miss all the good dresses."

I shrugged. "I would rather eat ice cream with you than fight my way through a crowd of crazed girls, who might end up ripping each other's dresses. I'm sure we'll find something we like later."

At that, a small smile appeared on Claire's lips. "You're right."

I hooked my arm with Claire's and took her to the ice cream shop. As I expected, the place was deserted. We ordered two scoops on a waffle cone each, and sat at the tall counter in front of the glass wall, watching the cozy streets outside.

"So ..." I started. This had been my plan all along: to get her to a nice place and have a long talk. "What's going on with you and Tanner?"

Claire almost dropped her cone. I thought she would evade my question, ignore me, rush out the shop, but instead, she surprised me by letting out a long breath and saying, "I honestly don't know."

"What do you mean?"

"I mean ... we're together and I love him. I know he can be rough and say bad things to me here and there, but then he turns around and treats me like a princess. But sometimes, only sometimes, I'm scared of him."

Admitting that to me must have been hard. I reached over and took her hand in mine. "If you're scared of him, it means there's something wrong there." There were a ton of wrong things in their relationship, but I was afraid that if I started drilling her about each of them, she would shut down again, and not talk to me anymore. "He needs to treat you like a princess all the time, not only sometimes."

"I know. I keep telling myself that, but it's so hard." She turned her green eyes to me. "I've actually considered breaking up with him a couple of times ..."

"Claire, you can do it," I said, taking advantage of her admission. "I know breaking up hurts, but you have to do it. And I promise to help you through it. I'll hold your hand like this the entire time." I squeezed her hand.

She offered me a sad smile. "When you put it like that."

"I know you can do it," I insisted.

Finally, she nodded. "All right. I promise to break up with him."

"Before the ball tomorrow," I added.

"Okay. I'll break up with him before the ball tomorrow night."

A sense of relief filled my chest. Having Claire away from Tanner was one last thing for me to worry about.

After we finished the ice cream, Claire and I went for a walk around the villa. After all, the main dress shop was probably still full, and I didn't want to have a catfight for a dress anytime soon.

In the end, that worked out quite well, as Claire and I stumbled by a small store at the edge of town, with the most beautiful gowns I had ever seen. And I found the perfect dress for me.

RANDALL HAD MADE IT CLEAR THAT HE WANTED ME TO GO TO the fucking Spring Hunter Ball tonight, but I wasn't in the mood. Though, I couldn't stay locked in my room either—not when knowing Erin would be there. So, I put on some shorts and thermal tee and went to the Hyacinth building, where I put up a sweat in the weight lifting room.

It was better this way. If I stayed here, I was getting a good workout, and I wouldn't have to see Erin, probably even more beautiful than usual, all dressed up for the ball.

I confess that I wanted to go just to see her.

But I couldn't. I wouldn't. I had already killed two people this month. I didn't want to put Erin in even more danger than she already was.

With the music blasting loudly through the ceiling speakers, I didn't hear anyone approaching me, until I heard his voice.

"I knew I would find you here."

I dropped the bar on its hooks and scooted from underneath it. I frowned at Harvey, who was dressed in a black tuxedo. "What the fuck are you doing here?"

"Saving you from your misery."

"My misery?"

"Don't pretend everything is fine and dandy," he said, slipping his hands inside his pants pockets. "You might not like it, but I know you, and I know you're here to keep yourself busy, to keep your mind busy, because you think you shouldn't go to the ball."

"That's not true—"

"No, it isn't the entire truth," he said, cutting me off. "The truth is that you're hiding from Erin, because you think you don't deserve her."

I stood from the bench, suddenly upset with the direction this conversation was taking. "I think you're wasting your time here, Harvey."

"Look," he started. "I know things have been messed up between us, and for some time there, I really hated you for all the things that happened ..." He was talking about how my dear, dead father had killed his uncle and maimed his mother to the point where she couldn't hunt anymore. "But with the recent events, I saw that I might be wrong about you."

This was so atypical. Harvey didn't do the whole mushy thing. "What the fuck are you getting at?"

"Just listen to me, dude," he snapped. "You just saved me from dying at the hands of an insane half-demon. I think I owe you at least some consideration." I stared at him, a little shocked. "During the past couple of weeks, I've been thinking a lot and I realized that I might have overreacted. You seem like a good guy, despite your heritage."

"So, in exchange for saving you, you're offering your friendship." I snorted. "No, thank you."

"Stop being a jerk and let me finish," Harvey said. "I'm not here to be friends again, idiot. I'm here to give you something in return, and that is the chance to tell Erin how you really feel."

"What the fuck?"

"I knew you would be here, holed up, licking your wounds, going insane inside your own mind, while in fact you should be out there, going after her, and confessing that you love her."

I stared at him. I hadn't allowed myself to think that word because I clearly didn't deserve it. If he thought he could tell me something like this, he was fucking wrong. "Harvey ..."

"I heard a bit of your argument with her that day," he continued. "You're trying to push her away because you're afraid of hurting her. Of getting her killed. Dude, I get it. I really get it. But you got to admit one thing: Erin is already in *a lot* of danger. Chances are that when her father comes for her, she'll end up dead. You know who could be by her side to help her? To protect her? You, you idiot."

Deep down, I knew he was right. But there were so many factors stopping me. How could I be there to protect her if there was a legion of demons after me? How could I keep her safe if Randall was most likely to use her against me? How would she be well if I brought pain and disgrace to a lot of people around me?

My head and heart were at war right now, and I wasn't sure who would win.

"It's not that easy," I said, my voice low. Dejected.

"It never is," Harvey said, sounding way older than his nineteen years. "But you got to keep going. If you let fear stop you, then why are you living? Come on, Rey. Erin likes you, and she'll be at the ball, waiting for someone to dance with her. That could be you."

Fuck.

I let out a long sigh, wishing I was stronger. But I wasn't. When it came to Erin, I could barely think straight. "All right." The words were surprising even to me. "I'll go to this fucking ball."

* * *

HARVEY DIDN'T WAIT FOR ME. HE SAID HE HAD TO HEAD TO THE ball, but if I didn't show up soon, he would drag me there. I believed him, so I hurried up. I took a shower, put on a tuxedo with a silver bow tie, combed the longer strands of my hair back, and went to the ballroom at the Aster building.

The place had always been grand and fancy, with a high ceiling, big thorn chandeliers, and large windows, but tonight, it was even fancier. Round tables with fine tablecloths and elegant white flower arrangements lined the ballroom. In one corner, the bar with long marble countertops and black chairs was open. On the other, a small dais had been set up.

Surrounded by the academy's professor and other staff, Randall stood on the dais, finishing his speech.

"Once again, I thank the Blackthorn Hunters for all they do for our community," he said, with a wide smile I knew was plastic. The crowd clapped enthusiastically, especially the full-fledged demon hunters. Randall raised his champagne glass high. "Let's honor them tonight."

The clapping intensified. He climbed down the dais and

turned to the professors, who congratulated him on a great event. Then he turned to the full-fledged hunters. Andre, Doreen, and Norah were among them.

Norah ... I had almost forgotten she had seen us helping Farrah escape, and she had let us go. I didn't understand why. Wasn't she brainwashed like the other demon hunters?

The band, located on a balcony upstairs, started playing. My attention moved elsewhere.

I scanned the area, searching for her.

For the woman who had stolen my heart long before she had claimed my soul.

The crowd spread out, going for the tables around the ballroom, or for the bar, or just hanging out in the open area in the middle—the dance floor.

Then I saw her.

Standing beside Ava, Harvey, Peter, and Harper to the side of the dance floor.

My breath caught.

She wore a one-shoulder dress with the most unique fabric I had ever seen. It started dark green and went down to her feet in a gradient to bronze, reminding me of the color of her eyes. The dress had a tight bodice, and a long, flowy skirt with a slit to her mid-thigh. When she turned to speak with Harper, her leg peeked from underneath her skirt ... holy fuck. I swallowed hard, trying to regain control over my body, but it was too fucking hard when she looked this gorgeous. This hot.

Her long black hair was half-up and half-down, with a thin golden thread wove between the strands. And even from here, from several feet away, I could see she was wearing makeup—smoky eyes and red lips.

I really wanted to claim those lips right now.

But first ... first I had a confession to make.

Mustering my courage, I walked up to her.

"Hey," I said, stepping into their circle. Instantly, Erin froze beside me.

"Good to see you," Harvey said with a wink.

I offered my hand to Erin. "Would you like to dance?"

Erin glanced at my hand.

Harper took Erin's hand and placed it in mine. "Of course, she would."

Before Erin could pull her hand away, I tightened my grip and tugged her to me. Then, I spun her away from her friends.

"What the hell are you doing?" she asked, her tone harsh. Even though she was in my arms and she had her hands on my shoulders, she was tense. Uncomfortable.

"I know you must be mad at me—"

"Must be?" She glared at me, her golden eyes bright. "You told me once and for all, to stay away from you. And now you want to dance? I don't get you."

"When you say it like that, I feel like I'm only twenty-two, and not a thousand."

"Maybe you should start acting your age."

I went for a joke. "Then I would have to act like the dead." She didn't crack a smile. Fuck. "Erin, I'm sorry. I never meant to be rude to you and hurt you, but ..." Why wasn't this easier? Because I knew she would be even madder the moment I admitted the truth. She would hate me for lying, but I would win her trust again. I would earn her forgiveness. "I have something to confess."

"Excuse me," Thierry said, halting right beside us and forcing us to stop.

Erin dropped her hands from my shoulders and took a large step back. "There you are."

I frowned.

He handed her a flute with what looked like champagne. "Sorry it took so long. There were a lot of people at the bar." Then, he smiled at me. "Thank you for keeping my date entertained while I was getting us some drinks." He put his arm around her waist.

Erin kept her eyes trained on the flute.

Jealousy rolled inside me, feeding the rage I didn't know was hiding under my skin. I had been too late. Erin was here with another man. The rage and the jealousy heated up inside me. I felt like taking Erin's arm and pulling her to me. Yelling at Thierry that he would never be anything to her, because she was mine. She was my soulmate. My twin soul.

But that behavior, that outburst would only hurt Erin more in the end.

So, I reined in my feelings. "You're welcome."

I stepped back and watched as Thierry took Erin away from me, too numb to move. It fucking hurt to see them together, but as much as I tried, I couldn't make my feet move. They were glued to the ground as my heart wilted away with jealousy.

A moment later, a figure halted by my side. I turned, ready to bitch, when I saw who it was.

"Professor Martha ..." I gulped down.

"I'll go directly to the point, Rey," she said, her eyes on the dance floor. "Stay away from Erin."

My jaw dropped. I forced it closed. "Why—"

Her head snapped and her eyes shone with something dark, something dangerous. "Don't try to hide it. I can see, as clear as day, the way you look at Erin."

I wasn't going to fall for this. "I think you're mistaken."

"Hear me out, Rey," Martha started, her voice low. Menacing. "I can take care of Erin. I don't need you to watch out for her. In fact, do me a favor: stay away from her. Her future is already too complicated to have you thrown in there and messing things up even more for her."

I gritted my teeth. "I didn't plan on getting close to her." What a lie.

She tsked. "Yeah, tell yourself that." Martha stepped right in front of me and pressed her finger on my chest. "Stay away from my daughter. That's the only warning I'm giving you." She plastered a fake smile on her face. "Now, if you'll excuse me."

Just like that, Martha walked away from me.

What the fuck had just happened? So now, besides all the other reasons I had to stay away from Erin, I had also been threatened by her mother? Was this for real.

It had been a mistake coming here. I had allowed the sliver of hope that was always in the back of my heart to come forth. I had allowed it to deceive me. And look where it got me. Now I felt stupid and heartbroken for seeing Erin with her date *and* for getting a fucking warning from her mother.

That was it. Done with this night, I turned around and marched away.

A hand closed around my upper arm. "Don't go yet."

I jerked free of Harvey's grip. "Don't start. I listened to you and look where that got me?"

"Dude, I didn't know she had agreed to come with Thierry. If I had, I wouldn't have said anything. I would have left you alone."

"Give me two minutes and I can be alone again."

Harvey shook his head. "No, not tonight. Since you're here, try to be a normal person for once."

"I'm not a normal person."

"That's why I said try." Harvey grabbed my arm again and pulled me back to Ava and Harper. I could have fought him and walked away, but I felt too exhausted even for that.

So I let him.

And regretted it five minutes later, when Erin and Thierry joined our circle. Thierry smiled wide, and Erin had a rose tint to her cheeks, as if she was either laughing too much, or drank too much.

I didn't know which one was worse.

Despite the overwhelming feelings inside me, I couldn't take my eyes off Erin ... and Thierry. She was stunning, but he wasn't bad either. They looked nice together. If he could love her in a way I couldn't, then maybe it was for the best. He was a good demon hunter, with a good heart. He would be able to protect her without bringing more danger into the mix.

I should be happy for her.

But I was fucking dying on the inside.

A moment later, Erin glanced around, a knot between her brow. "You guys haven't seen Claire?"

Harper shook her head. "I was just thinking about her. Why isn't she here?"

"We were heading this way together, then she said she forgot something and went back," Erin said. "I wanted to go back with her, but she knew I had to arrive early for one final check on the guest list and decorations, so she told me to go on, and that she would catch up with me."

"You got here a few minutes after me," Ava said. "And that was over an hour ago."

"I know. I'm worried," Erin muttered.

"I saw her going to the Snapdragon building when I was on my way here," Peter said.

Erin's shoulders squared. "I'm going after her."

I opened my mouth to tell her I would go with her, when Thierry offered her his arm. "I'll go with you."

With a small grin, Erin placed her hand on the inside of his arm.

It killed me to see them like that.

"Wait," Harper called. "Look."

We all turned to the entrance.

Claire walked into the ballroom with Tanner right beside her.

25

WHAT THE HELL? YESTERDAY CLAIRE HAD PROMISED SHE would break up with Tanner. As far as I knew, she hadn't seen him today.

And now she showed up late to the ball with him?

No one else in the ballroom seemed aware of how that irritated me, except for the people in our circle. That didn't stop me from marching past clueless students and stomping to her.

"What the hell is this?" I asked, pointing to her and Tanner.

Claire averted her eyes. "He's my date."

With a wide smile, Tanner took Claire's hand and pulled her closer.

I glared at him, then looked at my friend. "He's not your date. He's a jerk who is always mean to you. You said you would break up with him!"

Tanner let out an amused chuckle.

"Sorry, Erin," Claire muttered, still not looking at my eyes.

"I can't break up with him. I love him and I think we can work this out."

My jaw fell open. "You can't be serious."

Tanner winked at me. "You heard your friend. Now excuse me, because I'd like to dance with my date."

He tugged her past me.

"Claire!" I called, not believing what was happening.

"Sorry, Erin," she muttered as she disappeared into the crowd on the dance floor with Tanner.

I stayed planted in place, confused and extremely upset. What the hell was going on here? Why hadn't she broken up with him? How could he have this kind of power over her?

I took a step forward, intent on taking Claire away from Tanner, but Thierry showed up beside me and gently touched my arm. "I know you're worried about her, but it doesn't seem you'll be able to change her mind tonight. Why don't you try to enjoy the party? You can talk to her again tomorrow."

Thierry was probably right, but I couldn't wrap my mind around it. Why was she here with this douche? She should have come with me. Right at this moment, we could be arguing with Ava and flirting with Harvey. What was more fun than that?

Defeated, I let Thierry escort me back to the circle with our friends. Harper couldn't take her eyes off Claire, clearly as saddened as I was, though I didn't think the others noticed her real feelings.

Thierry did his best to distract me. He took me for a spin around the ballroom, and mingled with my friends, when I was sure he would have rather stayed with the other full-fledged demon hunters.

Besides not looking at Claire, I tried not looking at Rey too.

Such a damn hard task.

I could have sworn he wasn't coming to the ball. If he hadn't, it would have been so much easier. But the moment he came into the ballroom and danced with me, the wall I tried to build around my heart shook. It almost crumbled.

But I remembered the night he was a jerk to me, saying I had to let him go once and for all. I remembered how awful I felt. How lost. A little sadness snaked through my chest, mixing with anger and frustration. I grabbed on to those feelings and used them to keep the wall around my heart intact.

It certainly didn't help that he came in looking so dashing in the tuxedo and the silver tie that emphasized his pretty, shiny gray eyes. His hair had been combed slightly back, showing off more of his angular face. With his height, his sure steps, his lean shoulders, and how I knew his chest—and probably the rest of his body—was completely ripped, it was hard looking away. Staying away. Telling my heart to forget him.

Despite myself, I watched as he mingled, talking to professors and the guards that were stationed at strategic points. He also talked to the headmaster for a long while, until the headmaster exited the ballroom, then moved on to the bar where he ordered a beer.

Occasionally, his eyes met mine, but he averted his gaze. I really didn't get it. He made me so freaking confused. He told me to stay away from him, and tonight he had asked to dance with me. He had looked at me as if he worshipped me. It seemed he wanted to tell me something.

And then he quit. He let go and walked away.

I shook my head.

"You know," Thierry started, catching my attention. For a moment there, I forgot we were slowly gliding around the dance floor. "You've spent most of the night by my side. Even though your body is here with me, I can see your mind and heart aren't."

I stared at him, a little shocked and upset he had noticed it. "Thierry—"

"It's okay," he said quickly. "I'm a little jealous of Rey right now, but I'll be okay."

"I'm so sorry," I whispered, ashamed of myself. This wasn't right. I had agreed to be his date, and yet I spent the night looking at another man.

"It's okay, really." He stopped dancing. "In fact, to show you it's okay, I'm going to tell you this: go to him. Let him know how you feel."

I scrunched my nose. "I already did that. He rejected me."

Thierry frowned. "Then he's lying."

"What do you mean?"

"I've seen the way he looks at you. It's the same way you look at him. He might not acknowledge it, perhaps, but I'm sure he feels the same way you do."

Could it be? Could Rey be lying to me? I had considered that a thousand times, or more, but when he shut me out like that, I decided it couldn't be true.

But now even Thierry was telling me it was true.

"I don't know," I muttered.

"I understand your reservation, but I think that at least once, you should tell him straight how you really feel. Get it off your chest. All the right words. If he still rejects you ..." He shrugged. "Then it's his loss. But at least you can move on."

I stared at Thierry. Poor guy had been on a date with me a minute ago, and now he was pushing me toward another guy.

"I didn't mean for this to happen. I mean, us, this way. You're handsome and nice ... I was hoping to fall for you. I'm sorry I didn't."

He nodded. "Unfortunately, we can't control the matters of the heart. I know that." He picked up my hand and kissed the top. "Now go on, and good luck."

"Thanks."

I stayed in the same spot while Thierry walked away from me. I felt relieved he was so cool about all of this, but also ashamed it had taken this long for me to realize that no matter what I did, Rey wouldn't leave my heart so easily.

I inhaled deeply, calling the few threads of courage I still had within me to fill my veins, to give me strength. I was sure I would be rejected again, but this time, I was going to be honest.

This time, I would tell him I loved him.

I scanned the ballroom, searching for Rey. I found him at the bar, still nursing the same beer from before.

With determined steps, I walked to him.

I was about ten feet from him when he saw me. His gray eyes on me, he straightened and rested his drink on the bar counter.

Shit, he looked so freaking hot.

My heart beat so fast—from the anticipation, from the high, from the courage, and from the fear of what he could say to me—I was surprised no one else heard it, even over the loud music playing in the ballroom.

He frowned. "Erin, what is it? Something happened?"

I halted right in front of him. I opened my mouth and nothing came out. Flashes of all the times he pushed me away ran through my mind. What if this was a mistake?

Hadn't I made myself clear already? Didn't he know I liked him way too much?

It didn't matter. This would be the last time I bothered him with this. If he rejected me, I would surely, definitely walk away and never look back.

"I need to tell you something," I blurted out.

"About?" Rey asked, his voice low, the shine in his eyes guarded.

"Rey, I—"

"What the hell?"

His voice was like a grate scraping against my ears. My fist clenched. I turned around and found Tanner looming over a cowering Claire, a few feet from Rey and me.

"Please," Claire croaked with tears brimming in her eyes.

"I already told you, you're stupid," Tanner barked, his voice loud. More people were starting to take notice of what was going on.

"Tanner—"

The sound of the slap echoed through the ballroom. People stopped chatting and dancing, and even the band stopped playing.

And I fumed.

Ready to punch him in the face, I stomped to him.

But before I could lay a hand on him, Tanner turned to me. He sneered before his entire body shimmered.

I took a step back as his form changed right in front of my eyes. His hair grew long and spiky, his hazel eyes darkened and stretched, his mouth became a huge gap, full of pointy teeth. His tanned skin turned sickly green, and he gained at least a foot, if not more, causing his tuxedo to stretch and rip along his shoulders and legs.

As if on cue, dozens of garrimps swarmed the ballroom through the doors and windows.

Panic ensued.

Amid it all, Tanner, in his new form, pointed his long, thick finger at me. "I'm here for you."

26

MOST STUDENTS PANICKED WHILE THE DEMON HUNTERS summoned their Dawnblades and started battling the garrimps.

Holding my Dawnblade, I ran to Erin. I grabbed her hand and pulled her behind me. "Who are you?"

"I'm the one who will be honored for ages," Tanner snarled, his voice thick and loud. "Erin is a Demon Kissed Queen of the underworld, a demonic princess, and I've come here to kill her and gain King Brikan's favor."

Even though the battle in the ballroom was loud and messy, it was like there was a pause, when everyone heard and acknowledged what Tanner said.

Fuck, now everyone knew Erin was King Brikan's daughter.

I raised my sword. "Come and get her. It'll be your end."

Tanner let out a hollow laughter as Andre lunged at him, coming from behind him, but as if he had sensed a fly, Tanner swatted him away. Andre flew across the room, landing on top of the other hunters.

"Stop!" Erin yelled from behind me.

Tanner snarled. "Only if you come to me. Come to me and let me kill you."

As if I would ever allow that.

A few feet behind the demon, Claire cowered against an upturned table, her hand over her cheek, where Tanner had slapped her.

Tanner stared at Erin with his dark eyes. "I've tried approaching you, but you never even looked at me. So, I started playing with Claire instead. This way, I knew I could eventually get close to you. Besides, your friend was fun ... for a little while."

"You piece of shit!" Erin stepped forward, as if she would cut Tanner's throat. I held her wrist and kept her back.

With a wicked, sharp-tooth grin, Tanner opened his arms. "Come to me. I'm ready to kill you."

That was it. This fucking guy was dying right now.

Dawnblade raised, I lunged at Tanner. With a guttural snarl, Tanner bared his sharp-teeth and lifted his arms, showing off his fingers, which elongated into long, knife-like claws. He clicked them before swiping for me.

I skidded to a stop and leaned back, the tip of his claws whooshing past my chest. Half an inch closer, and he would have slashed across me.

Doreen and Norah jumped on Tanner's back. He fought them off with ease.

I took two steps back, trying to think how to reach for him before he reached for me.

A foot from my side, Erin extended her hand. I grabbed her wrist. "No, don't." She turned her golden eyes to me. "Don't call your Dawnblade. Not here with a room full of demon hunters."

"Why not?"

I shook my head once. "They won't like it, and who knows that they will do to you. This isn't the time. Fight with magic only."

An annoyed furrow fell between her brows. She wasn't happy, but she nodded.

Tanner let out a roar, and I turned to see the two demon hunters who had been fighting him flying across the ballroom. Behind Tanner, Claire finally got up and ran.

Beside me, Erin called her darkfire. She threw successions of bolts of darkfire at Tanner, but he moved his arms from side to side, cutting through the bolt as if they were made of air.

"What the hell?" Erin asked, the shock clear in her voice. "Were those his claws?"

I watched as Tanner zeroed in on Erin again. "I don't know, but it seems Tanner's best weapon is those claws."

Tanner took a slow step toward us, toward Erin, as if he wanted her to die of anticipation. I couldn't let him get to her. I charged, my sword poised.

As I expected, Tanner swiped his long arms and claws at me again. I ducked under them, my sword ready to strike his legs. But even though he was big, he wasn't slow. He spun fast and slapped my arm to the side with his claws. The grip on my sword loosened as an electrical shock ran up my arm and radiated into my shoulder. I was momentarily taken aback by his power and barely saw one of his hands coming down at me. I stepped back, but not fast enough. One of his nails scratched across my collarbone, and pain like the sting of electricity squeezed my chest.

Groaning and shaking, I fell to my knees.

"Rey!" Erin cried.

I couldn't move. I couldn't even respond to her, my motor control gone with Tanner's overwhelming power. From the corner of my eyes, I saw as Erin summoned her magic. With a scream, she released a big bolt of darkfire. It zipped to Tanner, but as before, he cut through him like paper.

Erin was ready, though. She sent one bolt after the next, in several directions and aiming at different places. Tanner was busy cutting through them all, until he finally missed.

The bolt hit his shoulder, pushing him back a couple of feet.

Tanner glanced at his shoulder and groaned. "That hurt!" He fixed his eyes at Erin. "You're dead now."

Snapping his teeth like a cannibal, Tanner rushed Erin. She summoned a wall of darkfire, but Tanner sliced through it and grabbed her shoulders.

"Erin! No!" I screamed, the words coming out in a croak. Desperation filled me. I willed the shock to leave me, my muscles to obey me, my strength to come back, but I could barely move my fingers.

Claire came forward, trying to reach Erin. Tanner chuckled. "You're so stupid," he snarled before slapping her aside. Claire tumbled to the ground and slid across the floor.

Erin fought against Tanner, but she yelped as he injected her with the same power he had used on me. Erin's body shook as he slammed her to the floor. Her head lolled to the side, as if she didn't have any more strength to fight.

As if she was dead.

My heart squeezed.

"Erin! Wake up!" I screamed. My hand finally moved.

Tanner lifted his big, ugly head and grinned with his sharp teeth. "I'll enjoy this." He poised his claws above her chest.

A few seconds ago, I could barely move my hand, but right at this moment? I found strength I didn't know I had and pushed to my feet. My muscles screamed against the faint shocks that still ran through my body, but I pushed through it.

For her, I would always push through.

I careened into Tanner, knocking him aside. Tanner turned his attention to me, but by then, I had already sliced through his chest.

"You think that's enough to kill me?" Tanner cried. He lifted his claws to me.

I leveled my sword, ready to cut through his claws, even if he shocked me from here to the underworld, but then the doors of the ballroom burst open and Randall marched in, followed by Vaira and the rest of his Black Knight Unit.

"Take this demon down!" Randall ordered.

The Black Knights, dressed in a dark uniform similar to the Blackthorn Hunters', charged the higher demon. I grabbed Erin's hand and pulled her back, before she and I were even more hurt amid the chaos.

With so many half-demons attacking him, plus the demon hunters, and a few brave students, Tanner didn't stand a chance. He fell to the floor with a loud thud.

Randall worked his magic and bound Tanner's arms, torso, and legs, tying them with magical vines that sprouted from thin air. Tanner roared and fought against them, but honestly, no one had the power to defeat Randall. By then, most of the garrimps had been killed. The ones still alive fled.

Randall halted beside a fallen Tanner. "He has been possessed," he announced. "We'll take him to the dungeons." Then, he turned to Erin and me. "You two are coming with me."

27

IN SILENCE, REY AND I FOLLOWED THE HEADMASTER AND THE rest of the Black Knight Unit as they carried a numb Tanner to the basement of the Aster building, where the dungeons were located.

Until a few minutes ago, I didn't know this building had a basement, much less a dungeon.

On the way there, Rey asked me if I was all right about three hundred times. I always told him I was, even though my hands still shook from the shock-like attacks, and my heart still raced from almost being killed.

We went through hidden doors, down a wide, but dark set of stairs, past a long corridor, and then into a wide room with several doors.

The headmaster opened one of the doors. "In here."

The handful of half-demons who were dragging Tanner went in the room. From the door, Rey and I watched as they deposited Tanner on a tall iron table in the middle of the room, where a wide black circle had been drawn on the stone floor. They strapped thick leather clamps around his legs, arms, and torso—the vines disappeared—then they retreated from the room.

"Come," the headmaster said to Rey and me as he entered the room.

I hesitated, but when Rey went in, I forced myself to move and walked in with him. The headmaster closed and locked the door behind us.

"What are you going to do?" Rey asked, his eyes trained on Tanner.

"This is an exorcism room," the headmaster said, approaching the iron table. "I'm going to strip the demon from Tanner's body."

"What will happen to Tanner?" I asked in a low voice.

"That will depend on him." The headmaster took off the jacket of his tuxedo. "If he's strong enough, he'll survive." He folded the sleeves of his shirt up. "Now, stay back. This can get messy."

Rey and I retreated to the wall beside the locked door.

At first, I tried following the ceremony. The headmaster started by summoning his power and chanting some words in what I believed was a demonic language. A small dagger appeared in his hand and he leaned over Tanner. He ran the dagger's tip across Tanner's shirt, exposing his stomach. Then he grazed the blade's tip over Tanner's skin—enough to scratch and draw droplets of blood.

Next, the headmaster moved to Tanner's arms. He repeated the same process.

How much blood did he need for this ceremony?

The squeak of a little mouse reached my ears three seconds before the headmaster fished out a white mass from his pocket. Holding it by the tail, the headmaster tugged the mouse high, while still chanting the same nonsense.

Then, he brought the dagger to the mouse and pierced him. The headmaster drew the dagger down, and blood pooled on Tanner's chest.

Feeling like I was going to be sick, I grabbed Rey's arm and buried my face in his upper arm. If I kept my eyes closed, maybe, just maybe, I wouldn't register what was happening. Maybe, just maybe, I wouldn't remember any of this later.

"Here he comes," the headmaster called.

I spied over Rey's shoulders. A dark shadow emerged from Tanner's mouth. A thick cloud that traveled up and swirled close to the ceiling. The shadow pushed against the invisible walls of the circle on the floor, and shrieked each time, as if it hurt. Finally, it came back to the rough stone floor, where it took shape. Even though it didn't have Tanner's features anymore, it was easy to see the demon who had possessed him and used his body. It had the same large build, the same greenish skim, the same dark eyes, the same gaping mouth.

And the same gaze that zeroed in on me.

Rey took my hand in his.

The headmaster summoned his Dawnblade. "State your name!"

"You can't keep me in here," the demon snarled before pushing against the circle's power again. It shrieked and retreated to the center of the circle.

"I guess I can," the headmaster said. "Now, state your name."

"I'm Orzon," the demon said. He twisted around, as if the words were being pulled out of him. Like magic. Was this some power from the containment circle? "I came here to kill Erin and gain the favor of King Brikan."

"Why did you possess Tanner?" the headmaster gesture to Tanner, who was still lying on the iron table.

I didn't want to acknowledge how he looked right now.

"I couldn't get into the academy by myself," the demon said with a bite. "I needed a body to carry me. This boy crossed my path and I took him."

The headmaster twirled his dark Dawnblade in his hand. "Anything else I should know before I kill you?"

"I won't go down without a fight," the demon snarled.

"As I hoped."

His sword held high, the headmaster ran into the circle.

Orzon's fingers turned into the same knife-like claws from before. But even a demon like him wasn't a match for the headmaster. With his crude Dawnblade—so similar to mine —the headmaster slashed through his claws. The demon let out a roar that shook the walls. Using his magic, the headmaster immobilized the demon. Orzon roared again, trying to move but unable to.

The demon's scream choked in his throat when the headmaster pierced the demon's chest with his Dawnblade. Magic spread through the demon's torso in light and dark lines, around his shoulders, up his neck.

The demon shrieked as he was burned from the inside out.

A moment later, Orzon exploded in a cloud of black smoke.

The headmaster waved his hand and the cloud was gone. His sword disappeared too. Smoothing his shirt, he turned to us. "The demon is gone."

"What about Tanner?" Rey asked.

The headmaster shrugged. "He wasn't strong enough."

Oh no.

Sadness overwhelmed me. Tanner had been a pest these past couple of months, but it was only because Orzon had possessed him. I bet he wasn't a bad guy before. And now he was dead.

"What do we do now?" Rey asked.

"Take his body away," the headmaster said, as if we were taking out the trash. "I'm going back to the ballroom to appease the masses and clean up the mess." He turned his eyes to me. "Meanwhile, stay quiet. Now everyone knows about you and there will be repercussion."

"Should I be scared?" I asked, already scared. I hadn't planned on hiding what I was and whose child I was forever, but I also hadn't planned for everyone to find out so soon.

"We'll deal with it," the headmaster said.

Without another look at us, he walked out of the room.

Rey and I exchanged a glance.

"Are you okay?" he asked, his voice soft. Caring.

So much had happened in the last hour or so, my mind was still trying to play catch up. And my feelings ... I was mostly numb on the inside.

"I don't know," I admitted. "I just want to get this night over with."

He nodded. "Then we better take Tanner's body to the infirmary." Rey left the room in a hurry. I froze, suddenly alone with a body in an exorcism room where a higher demon had been killed. A moment later, Rey came back carrying what looked like a stretcher and a gray blanket. "I found this in another room."

It wasn't easy, but thankfully demon hunters had

increased strength. Like me, students might develop it slowly, but with my half-demon side, it balanced out.

Rey and I put Tanner's body on the stretcher, covered it with the blanket, and carried him out of the dungeons and the Aster building, across the courtyard, and into the Daffodil building, where the infirmary was located.

We had barely stepped inside when Claire showed up.

"What are you doing here?" I asked, surprised.

"I want to help," she said, her voice as heartbreaking as her downcast expression.

What could she help with? All we had to do was leave his body in one of the hospital beds, and be done. There was nothing more we could do for poor Tanner.

I opened my mouth to tell her to wait outside, because honestly, I didn't want her to see Tanner like this, but Rey was faster.

"Okay," he said. "Come on."

She hurried to my side and helped me with my end of the stretcher. Together, we went to the back room and laid Tanner in one of the beds.

"Shouldn't we call Cecile so she can come do something about him?" I asked, not comfortable leaving a body alone like that. Shouldn't he be put in a morgue, or whatever?

"I'll call her," Rey said. He fished his phone from inside his pocket.

I frowned at him. "I thought cell phones were forbidden at the academy," I said, going for a teasing tone. It didn't sound right.

"Usually, I don't carry it with me, but in all honesty, most students carry theirs all the time," Rey said.

"That's true," Claire said. "They just hide it well."

"What the hell are you talking about cell phones when there's a dead body to care for?"

Claire yelped. I blanched. Rey summoned his Dawnblade.

Opening his eyes, Tanner sat up and raised his hands. "Don't kill me!"

28

REY

I angled my Dawnblade to Tanner's throat. "Who are you?"

"It's okay," Tanner said, his eyes wide at my sword. "It's me. Orzon is gone now and it's just me."

I lowered my sword a little.

"H-how aren't you dead?" Erin asked. After the exorcism ceremony, I was curious about that too.

"I'm actually half-demon," Tanner explained. He grabbed a cloth from the bedside table and dabbed at the cuts across his chest. The blood had dried already, but I wondered how the fuck he wasn't dead from blood loss.

Erin brought a hand to her amulet. "It's warning me about you now. Why didn't it warn me before?"

I frowned. "I don't know."

"Perhaps because Orzon was able to overthrow the amulet's powers?" Tanner shrugged. "Anyway, I was able to slow down my heart rate enough so Randall would think I was dead."

"Why?" I asked, not understand. "Why not just wake up after the ceremony and walk out with us?"

Tanner turned in the bed, his legs hanging on the side. He pulled at his torn shirt, trying to hide his bare chest and his injuries, then he let out a long breath. "It's a long story." He fixed his eyes on Erin. "I'm not only a half-demon, but I'm a demonic prince, like you."

"You mean ..." Erin gasped.

Tanner nodded. "Yeah, I'm your half-brother. King Brikan is my father."

"That still doesn't explain why you were hiding," I prompted him.

"I found out I was the son of King Brikan last semester, so I spent winter break researching it," he said. "I found out there was a demon that knew all about it. All you had to do was pay his price." He let out a sigh. "It was a trick. I went to the demon and he possessed me. When he was inside me, he didn't find out who I was, or rather whose child I was, but he did find out about you, Erin. He became obsessed with killing you for King Brikan." He turned to Claire. "I'm sorry for everything I've done to you. I remember everything from when he was inside me, but I had no control over it. All the bad things I did were Orzon's doing. I'm so sorry, really."

Claire's lower lip trembled. "I'm actually relieved it wasn't you."

Tanner frowned. "I know you like me, or rather the other Tanner, but ..."

"You don't like me," Claire said, nodding. "I get it; don't worry." She attempted to smile, but it was clearly forced. "I forgive you."

"Thanks," he whispered. "And to finally answer Rey's question ..." Tanner looked at me. "I decided to take advantage of the fact everyone thinks I'm dead. This way I can leave the academy and research the Demon Kissed Queens prophecy."

Erin's eyes rounded. "You know about that?"

He nodded once. "I found out when Orzon took the book from the restricted section in the library and destroyed it. We'll have to find another one to discover more about the prophecy." He paused, growing more serious. "I want us to team up to take down King Brikan, eventually."

I frowned, not sure about this. What if Tanner was fucking lying about all of this? What if he was working for King Brikan? Or even Randall?

But what if he was telling the truth? Then, we would have some sort of secret weapon when the time came.

Erin hesitated. "I would like that."

I decided to trust her choice.

"Great," Tanner said. "You'll make a fine queen of the underworld."

Erin shook her head. "No, I don't want that. I'll help you take down King Brikan, if we can, but I don't want to be a queen. If you want, you can have the throne for yourself. After all, you're his son too."

"I confess the idea doesn't appeal to me either, but I think we can decide on the details later," Tanner said. "Now, I should leave the academy before someone else sees me."

"We'll help you out," I said.

The four of us headed out of the infirmary and into the darkness of the night behind the buildings. With my authority, I easily distracted the guards from one of the outposts while Tanner fled. He promised to keep in touch before disappearing into the mountain behind the academy.

In silence, Claire, Erin, and I made our way back to the dorm buildings.

"What is going to happen now?" Erin asked, her voice low. "They all know who I am. Perhaps I should have fled with Tanner."

I opened my mouth to tell her I wouldn't let anything happen to her, when a mob came out from beside the Snapdragon building and surrounded us—several of the professors, staff, and full-fledged demon hunters.

"You're a half-demon, daughter of King Brikan, a demonic princess, and a Demon Kissed Queen," Professor Graham shouted. "You deserve to die."

29

ERIN

I WAS DRAGGED INTO THE SCHOOL BOARD ROOM—WHICH looked like a round courtroom—in the Aster building, and thrown in front of the entire school board and staff. Professors, secretaries, officers, and even guards filled the chairs.

To add to the wound, the full-fledged hunters who had been at the ball were now in the room too.

And all of them were agitated and arguing about what to do with me.

In the back of the room, Rey stood, watching me with worried eyes. He had tried defending me when they surrounded me and took me away, but he had been one against many.

The headmaster took the chair behind the high desk behind me, while my mother was among the others, yelling at them in my favor. She would end up outed as my mother, which would only make things bad for her too.

I tried catching her eye to tell her to let it go, but she didn't even glance my way while she told them it wasn't my fault I had been born with the king of the underworld as a father.

Someone brought up the fact that I had helped Farrah escape from the demon hunters—how the hell did they find out about that?—and this time, Thierry was the one to shout I had been naive and easily swayed.

I didn't know if his comment helped or made me feel worse.

Norah, the demon hunter who helped us with Farrah, also spoke up in my defense, though she didn't make me feel stupid. She said they were mistaken about me, and that she vouched for me. That was quite touching considering I barely knew her.

Finally, the headmaster stood up and said, "Silence!" The room quieted in three seconds flat. "I understand this is a sensitive situation. We'll deal with it with the utmost care." He sat back down. "We'll listen to Erin, then to others who would like to state their opinion about the matter. At the end of this session, I'll make a decision." He gestured to me. "Erin, start."

I gulped, suddenly nervous with all eyes were on me. More than that, my fate was going to be decided in the next few minutes. I could be thrown out of the academy, or killed, or worse.

I inhaled deeply and started, "I didn't know I was the supreme demon's daughter until a few months ago. I don't feel any different from before and I think that if I had never found out, nothing would have changed. I'm not evil, and I'm not on the side of the demons. My destiny is to kill King Brikan and to take the underworld from him. Isn't that what all demon hunters want?"

"Who says you're not tricking us?" Kaitlin said. I had seen the female demon hunter during the ball's preparations. "You're here pretending to be good, just so we lower our guard. Then, you'll attack and King Brikan will destroy us."

"I say we should consider another game," Professor Graham said. "You could very well just kill King Brikan, then take the underworld for yourself. Who says you won't be worse than he is?"

"You're all looking way down the line," Professor Wesley said. "She's a half-demon, and that already warrants her death sentence."

"Then we have to talk about all the other half-demons who swarmed the ballroom this evening," Professor Eleanor said. She glanced at the headmaster. "Randall, care to explain?"

Randall looked at her as if she was the gum stuck to the sole of his shoe. But eventually, he responded. "I've created a group of half-demons, called the Black Knight Unit, and they were the ones who saved you tonight, if you don't recall. As Erin pointed out, not all half-demons are evil, and I believe we can integrate them into our society."

The protests escalated until they became a continuous roar inside the board room.

"They all have to die!" I heard among the shouts.

"She has to at least be thrown out the academy."

"Torture them! They must know secrets we don't."

I was shocked about how horrible these people were, how many cruel thoughts they had in their minds. Did they only see black and white? There were no shades of gray when it came to supernaturals?

"Silence!" the headmaster called again. This time, it took

longer for the people to quiet down. "I've made a decision. Erin Delman will stay in the academy, under my protection. She'll train with all of you so that she can help us take down the underworld when the time comes. Moreover, the Black Knight Unit will continue." He stood. "This meeting is now over."

The professors and demon hunters still protested as Randall walked to me, and after grabbing my arm, escorted me out of the room.

He took me to the doors opening to the courtyard. "Go directly to your room and lay low for the rest of the weekend. Things will probably be tough for you for a while."

I nodded.

The headmaster spun and walked away before I could thank him for sticking up for me and letting me stay at the academy. I heard the loud footsteps and the angry voices coming down the stairs, and I hurried out of the Aster building.

By now, it was the middle of the night, and all the students had been sent to bed hours ago, so I didn't encounter anyone as I ran to the Gardenia building.

I breathed in relief as I made it to the lobby safely.

"Erin."

I turned around as Rey walked into the building. "Hey. What are you doing here?"

"I just wanted to check on you," he said, his voice and eyes soft. What the hell was he doing? This was too confusing for me. "That was crazy and I thought—"

I steeled myself, knowing what would happen here. He would reel me in and then cast me out like a dead fish. "It's okay, Rey. I'm okay. You can go now."

Gray eyes turning silver, Rey ran a hand over his hair. "Fuck ..."

It happened too fast. One moment he was standing three feet from me, the next, I was pressed against the wall. Rey was right on top of me, his body glued to mine, his hands on my waist, and his lips crashing on mine.

I froze for a moment, at a loss of what to make of this moment. But before I could try to think this through, I melted into him. I sank into his soft, warm lips, into his deep, longing kiss, into his tongue that teased mine, that provoked me. Heat spread through my body as his hands traveled low, around my hips. Lost in the moment, I hooked a leg around his hips. My dress's slit exposed my leg, and Rey's hand smoothed across my bare skin.

I moaned against his lips, and he groaned against mine.

This ... this was paradise. This was perfect. This was meant to be.

If Rey wasn't my soul bond, then how could I feel like this? How could he ignite such a flame inside me? How could his kiss and his body fit mine so well?

As if hearing my thoughts, Rey groaned again and shifted his weight, aligning his hips with mine better, making me gasp with pure desire.

I grabbed the collar of his shirt, barely noticing they had been torn into pieces. Oh, yes, it had been during the fight against Tanner, or rather Orzon. I had seen that Tanner had struck him hard at least twice during the fight, but after all the craziness that came after, I had forgotten to check on him. I slipped my fingers under his torn shirt, caressing his skin, feeling a nasty scratch over his collarbone.

Worry about how badly injured Rey was overcame my

desire, and I broke the kiss. I tugged at his shirt and stared at his chest.

The wound wasn't too bad. It was a nasty scratch, but with the right ointment, it should heal nicely.

What made my heart skip a beat—or four—was the mark above his heart.

The soul bond.

Rey had the twin soul bond mark.

"Fuck. Erin—"

"You have the mark," I whispered, suddenly overwhelmed with emotion. I glanced up at his eyes, so silver tonight, and felt them pulling me in. "You're my twin soul."

"Erin," he whispered. A groan ripped from his throat as he dropped me fast and retreated several steps.

As if he had awoken from a spell, Rey whispered, "I'm sorry."

I frowned. "For?"

"For ... kissing you and holding you."

I wasn't following it. "Why are you sorry for that?"

"Because it shouldn't have happened. You shouldn't have seen the mark. I was doing such a good job hiding it before."

It took me a moment to process it all. "Wait. You just kissed me and now you're pushing me away again? I don't get it."

He ran a hand over his hair. "Erin, this is complicated."

I crossed my arms and held on to the rage simmering inside me before I broke down and cried in front of him. "Then make it uncomplicated by explaining it to me."

He let out an exasperated sigh. "I hid the mark before because I'm just trying to keep you safe, Erin. That's all I want. To keep you safe. Forever. And to do that, I have to stay away from you."

"Bullshit!"

He shook his head. "It's true. Everyone who gets close to me ends up dead. Even the ones who really don't want to get close to me. I don't want that to happen to you."

"So you're going to deny we are soulmates because you're scared I'm gonna get hurt? If I read between the lines, that means you like me." He averted his eyes. "You like me," I whispered, not sure if I was upset that he had hid it and lied to me, or happy that he was the one for me, and that he felt the same as I did. "Just think about that. Just like me. Just be with me."

I hated the pleading tone of my voice—I was *not* a girl who begged for a guy to like her, but come on! He already liked me. He was my soulmate. Why didn't he give in and be with me?

As if warding himself against me, Rey took another step back. "We can't, Erin. There are too many factors moving against us. We can't be together."

I stared at him, disappointed. "So you're giving up on me, on the unique bond we share, because of problems you won't even share with me? Sorry, but it sounds like you're hiding something shady and using any idiotic excuse to push me away."

"It's best if you think that," he said, his voice deadpan.

So, that was how it would go. He went back to being the jerk from the beginning of the semester, and I went back to being the lovesick girl who pined for him every second of the day.

I was done.

I was so freaking done.

"Have it your way," I said.

Heartbroken, I climbed the stairs and went into my room.

Still dressed in the pretty dress, with my hair half-done, and makeup—probably a little smeared—I threw myself onto bed, hugged my pillow, and promised myself I wouldn't cry over him.

What a big, fat lie.

30

I LEFT THE GARDENIA BUILDING WITH MY TAIL TUCKED BETWEEN my legs and my heart in my hand. I knew I had hurt Erin badly, but it was for the best. I knew it was.

To drive my point home, she had almost died tonight again. It didn't matter if it was because of me or not. She would be in even more danger beside me, and I couldn't accept that.

How fucking stupid I had been? Kissing her like that? I had no fucking self-control. And now the problem was, every time I thought about kissing her, about her lips on mine, about my body pressed against hers, I wanted more. I needed more.

But I couldn't have it.

I also couldn't stay here. Since choosing me, Randall always commented on how I would graduate and start working at the academy as a professor. He wanted me close, so I could learn everything—all lies, of course. Randall didn't fool me. He might look like a deity to everyone else, but I knew his soul wasn't pure. It didn't matter what he wanted. I *needed* to get away from here. Following my instinct, I turned toward the Aster building, intent on knocking on Randall's office this late at night and talking to him. He had to hear me out. He had to understand. I would beg, if I had to, to be sent to some full-fledged demon hunter outpost, preferably far away from here. There were plenty of outposts located around the world. I was sure he could find a fit for me somewhere.

I was almost at the entrance of the building when Professor Crimson stepped in my way.

"Professor," I said, stopping before him. "What's the matter?"

"I have a deal to offer you," he said simply.

Another deal? I had plenty of those to go around already. "I'm not interested." I walked around him.

"I know about the soul bond," he said.

I stilled. "What did you say?"

"I know you and Erin Delman share a soul bond."

Slowly, I turned around. "How the fuck do you know that?"

"I won't reveal my secrets to you," Crimson said, his tone superior, as if he liked playing with me. "Will you listen to me now?"

I didn't want to, but did I have any choice? I crossed my arms. "Go ahead."

"Randall has gone too far," Crimson said, his dark green eyes burning with fury. "Half-demons inside the academy? That's absurd." Apparently, he had found out about the soul bond, but not that I was also a half-demon. "I think it's time for a change, and I want you to help me with that."

I frowned. "What do you mean?"

"You'll help me take Randall down," he said. "Discredit him, throw him in the dungeons, kill him, whatever, so long as I'm the new headmaster by the end of the year."

I pondered this. Crimson wasn't any better than Randall in my opinion. At least, Randall was powerful enough that he could protect the academy and its students.

As for the soul bond. Whatever. Erin had already found out about it. What if everyone else did? It wouldn't change anything.

I shrugged. "That's not my problem. Find someone else to help you."

"I don't think I made myself clear," Crimson said, his voice gaining a harsh tone. "If you don't help me, or if you tell Randall about this plan, I'll kill Erin."

My heart stopped. "What the fuck?"

"What? She's a half-demon, the daughter of the king of the underworld. I bet I can easily implicate her and have her executed right here." He gestured to the courtyard with the Blackthorn tree. "Are you willing to risk that?"

"You're bluffing."

"Am I? Don't you know what I'm capable of?"

Oh, I knew. He might not show his claws in public, and most of the time, he looked pathetic when arguing with Randall, but I was sure Crimson would go to any lengths for his goals.

This couldn't be happening. How did I get out of one demonic contract, then find myself in another magical deal, and now be threatened into another one?

Fuck my life.

At least, this deal with Crimson wouldn't be magical, as

he had no magic like Randall, but with Erin on the line, did I dare play with it?

No, I didn't.

"What exactly do you want me to do?"

A wicked grin spread over Crimson's lips. "It's simple. Next semester, you'll be working as a professor after your graduation, just as planned. Meanwhile, you'll help me take Randall down."

"And Erin will be safe?"

He nodded. "I won't touch one single hair on her head."

That didn't bring me the assurance I was looking for, but I doubted I would get more from him.

Without a choice, I said, "Fine. I'll help you."

Triumphant, Crimson extended his hand to me. "Great." I reluctantly shook his hand. "It's a deal." He took a step back. "I'll talk to you soon."

I watched, rooted to the ground, as Crimson turned around and practically sauntered away.

What the fuck just happened? I had been on my way to convince Randall to send me away from the academy so I could be away from Erin, and now I had my hands tied and couldn't leave even if I wanted to.

My mind worried about Erin even more now. Before I was afraid Randall would use her against me, and that was exactly what Crimson was doing. And I knew he wouldn't waste an opportunity to press me on my task, by threatening her —or even acting on it.

This was all fucked up.

Besides being concerned about Erin, I also worried about the future of the academy. For Erin's sake, I would help Crimson. I would find a way for him to steal Randall's throne. But what then? Would the academy and the students be safe in Crimson's hands?

I seriously doubted it.

I'M TORTURING OUR HEROES, AM I NOT? FRET NOT! THINGS GET better on the next book, *The Soul Bond*, which you can grab now by clicking here!

THANK YOU

Thank you for reading *The Hunter Secret*!

Reviews are very important for authors. If you liked my book, please consider leaving a review on your favorite retailer and/or on goodreads, please!

You can get the next book in the series now:

The Soul Bond

Don't forget to sign up for my Newsletter to find out about new releases, cover reveals, giveaways, and more!

If you want to see exclusive teasers, help me decide on covers, read excerpts, talk about books, etc, join my reader group on Facebook: Juliana's Club!

ABOUT THE AUTHOR

While USA Today Bestselling Author Juliana Haygert dreams of being Wonder Woman, Buffy, or a blood elf shadow priest, she settles for the less exciting—but equally gratifying—life as a wife, a mother, and an author. She resides in North Carolina and spends her days writing about kick-ass heroines and the heroes who drive them crazy.

Subscribe to her mailing list to receive emails of announcement, events, and other fun stuff related to her writing and her books: www.bit.ly/JuHNL

For more information:
www.julianahaygert.com

facebook.com/julianahaygert

twitter.com/juliana_haygert

instagram.com/juliana.haygert

goodreads.com/juliana_haygert

pinterest.com/julianahaygert

bookbub.com/authors/juliana-haygert

ALSO BY JULIANA HAYGERT

To find links and more info, go to:

www.julianahaygert.com/books/

Shorts

Into the Darkest Fire

Standalones

Daughter of Darkness

Rite World: Blackthorn Hunters Academy

The Demon Kiss (Book 1)

The Hunter Secret (Book 2)

The Soul Bond (Book 3)

The Shadow Trials (Book 4)

The Infernal Curse (Book 5)

Rite World

The Vampire Heir (Book 1)

The Witch Queen (Book 2)

The Immortal Vow (Book 3)

The Warlock Lord (Book 4)

The Wolf Consort (Book 5)

The Crystal Rose (Book 6)

The Wolf Forsaken (Book 7)

The Fae Bound (Book 8)

The Blood Pact (Book 9)

The Wyth Courts

Winter King (Book 1)

Spring Warrior (Book 2)

Summer Prince (Book 3)

Autumn Rebel (Book 4)

The Fire Heart Chronicles

Heart Seeker (Book 1)

Flame Caster (Book 2)

Sorrow Bringer (Book 3)

Earth Shaker (Novella)

Soul Wanderer (Book 4)

Fate Summoner (Book 5)

War Maiden (Book 6)

The Everlast Series

Destiny Gift (Book 1)

Soul Oath (Book 2)

Cup of Life (Book 3)

Everlasting Circle (Book 4)

Willow Harbor Series

Hunter's Revenge (Book 3)

Siren's Song (Book 5)